Long Jetty Short Stories 1

Also by Sean Crawley and published by Ginninderra Press
Dead People Don't Make Jam

Sean Crawley

Long Jetty
Short Stories 1

Before the 'Rus

Long Jetty Short Stories 1: Before the 'Rus
ISBN 978 1 76109 313 5
Copyright © Sean Crawley 2022
Cover image: Sean Crawley

First published 2022 by
GINNINDERRA PRESS
PO Box 3461 Port Adelaide 5015
www.ginninderrapress.com.au

Contents

Bush Week

It's unlikely you'd ever meet Seamus O'Reilly at a social event. But if you did and you asked him what he did for a living, he'd answer, 'Barista.' And if you asked where, he would tell you, 'The Obsidian Tambourine in Long Jetty.'

You wouldn't ask any further questions because Seamus repels social interaction. He has a blank face and an awkward posture. He is impenetrable, appearing both uninteresting and uninterested at the same time. So you'd end up having to have to take over the conversation by perhaps remarking how dramatically Long Jetty has transformed over recent years. Seamus would listen and nod. Let you talk to the point where you would feel the awkward one. He would never ask you where you work, or ask anything about you. You'd finish your drink and use that as an excuse to move on.

If on the other hand you came over to me and introduced yourself, I could tell you about Seamus. I know lots about him. I have a file with his name on my laptop. But I wouldn't tell what I know about him, I do have some ethics. Besides, the investigation is continuing, ongoing, unresolved – his file is active. I know what he had for breakfast this morning, and what he wrote on his computer before that breakfast, and who he texted the night before that, and so on. And I record all of this in a report while I watch Seamus making coffee for myself and others who frequent the Obsidian Tambourine.

The investigation has been going on for months now. Seamus knows how I like my espresso. I'm there everyday he works and though he has never asked what I do for a living, I have told him I'm a writer. It's the best cover I could think of to explain my regular attendance at his workplace.

'I'm writing a collection of short stories,' I told him. 'I'm struggling with a connecting theme to tie them all together, because my (pretend) agent insists that the (imaginary) publisher who has expressed interest in my (non-existent) short stories wants a themed collection and not some hotchpotch of eclectic tales.'

Seamus handed over my cappuccino and nodded. Not a word.

Ethically and professionally, I should never have become friends with Seamus. My employers didn't need to remind me of that fact, but they did. Keep your distance, they said. And who are they? I've never met or spoken to any of them. They work for some special branch of something. And what is that something? It's either the government itself, or one of its intelligence agencies, or perhaps it's simply the federal police. I don't know. I'm a freelancer. All communication is online, encrypted messages exchanged in a dropbox that they remotely installed on my laptop. There are no emails, nor any form of mobile phone communication. If shit happens, like Seamus getting killed, or me being found out by someone, the only knowledge anyone could extract from me is that I work for a well organised and well paying branch of something or other. They are safe.

Seamus and I are at a poetry slam at the recently revamped Savoy picture theatre. The drinks cost a pretty penny and the poetry is uncomfortably personal. I don't get it. Neither does Seamus.

'What is this?' I ask Seamus while we take a piss in a break between poets.

'Bush week?'

'God, I haven't heard that for a long time. My grandmother used to say it when she babysat me and my brother.'

'I'm going home.' That's exactly how he says it. Man of few words.

'Yeah, sure. Have a good night, Seamus. I'm going to stay for a bit.' There is a person of interest that I need to check out.

From the windows, I watch Seamus cross the main road and walk up Thomson Street to where he lives.

I laugh to myself. What is this? Bush week? It's a funny saying. But then again, it's not that funny at all. It's a statement of disapproval. I imagine writing in my next report how I attended a poetry night with Seamus, thus revealing to them at the special branch of something or other that I've gone against orders and become a friend of the subject of my surveillance. I imagine their encrypted response: 'You've become friends? Didn't we advise that this would be undesirable? What do you think this is? Bush week?' Lots of rhetorical questions. Lots of disapproval.

The person of interest is a girl. She's at the bar. Guess I'll have another beer. I stand next to her. She orders a Negroni. She is checking her phone as the barmaid makes the drink. She writes a text. It's a bit of a blur, but has she written the name Seamus?

'What are the Negronis like here?' I interrupt.

She looks at me. I know the look. It screams, You're a creep and you don't stand a chance, bucko!

'Good.' That's it. That's her reply. One word. No eye contact. She moves off.

I order a beer.

I see this girl often at the Obsidian Tambourine. I have taken a picture of her and dropped it online in the box for them. They don't know her. But her regular appearance at Seamus's workplace, and my observation, which I reported, that one day she handed him what appeared to be a folded piece of paper, resulted in a direct instruction: 'Get a photo.' Now, I have an order to find out who she is. Not good. I thought the job was to remotely observe and report on Seamus O'Reilly. Now I have to engage with some woman. Definitely, not good.

I head back to the poetry slam upstairs. It's kicking off again. I spot the girl with the Negroni, which is not hard since she has this large head of red ringlets. There's no way I'm going to sit anywhere near her. She has already judged me and disapproved. I go back to where I was sitting with Seamus earlier. I click my fingers along with the crowd. I blend in and watch.

A large girl is at the mic and she riffs on about being fat. She calls herself that, fat. No one else can call her that. Oh, my God, I'm starting to slam. The spoken rhythms and rhymes are hijacking my brain. I tune out and focus back on the girl who thinks I tried to crack onto her at the bar. She is on her phone again, two thumbs texting. Did she actually type Seamus before? Did I really see her handing Seamus a piece of folded paper? And if my observation was correct, could that piece of paper have simply been something she found on her table? Something that she handed in out of a sense of doing the right thing? Did she say to Seamus, 'I found this on the table. I think it might be important and someone might come back for it'? And without hearing the verbal exchange, I report the incident and now must spy on this girl, who in all likelihood is nothing other than a regular attendee at the Obsidian Tambourine. And there's plenty of those.

The beer is a schooner. It's my third for the night. Seamus and I had a shout before he left. Now I'm drinking solo, and the ethanol is doing its magic. Evil magic. The girl with the mane of ringlets is sporadically checking her phone. I'm going to find out who she is. Her earlier judgement and dismissal will not deter me. She may be a relevant connection or maybe not. Either way, I will pursue her and find out who she is. She has become a challenge. I will prove her assessment of me as wrong. I will have her asking me, 'How are the beers at this place?' She will want to know me, know everything about me. Whereas I only want to know if she has some connection with Seamus and his past. I will not be what she initially assumed – some dude wanting to get into her pants.

The host of the poetry slam has a man bun. A wannabe hipster. Man buns are so yesterday. I'm getting critical – no, worse, cynical. The beer can do that. He is actually quite humorous and personable. He introduces the next act, an Indigenous man, well known for his powerful slamming. The crowd applaud as though they know this fella personally. Perhaps they do, perhaps everyone here tonight belongs to some tight little clique of local people into the arts, into poetry, into all sorts of existential misery and their contemporary modes of expression. The poet steps up to the mic, pulls back his hoody, and starts with a string of confronting truths. Click, click, click goes the crowd. This ain't no self-indulgent misery. He talks of mothers and fathers, sisters and brothers, aunties, uncles, blood and disease, and a history of story that started on the very first sunrise. I forget about the girl on the other side of the room checking her phone.

Something inside me is dissolving. And something else is awakening. The first poem ends. I want more. I want this truth. I want it in my face. Everything else is bullshit. The spying job, the pretending to be a short story writer, the desire to prove the Negroni girl wrong. Everything in this world is upside down and fucked up, big time. It's not bloody bush week, it's a full blown era of craziness!

And what is worse than all, is me becoming a friend of Seamus. Despite the cold hard facts recorded on the briefing that I was sent after accepting this job, outlining what he had done in the past and how far he fell, I like him. I like his taciturn manner. I like his simple life that I know so well. He doesn't deserve to be under surveillance by them from the department of something or other. One day out of the blue, Seamus said he wanted to read one of my short stories. I won't be able to hold that off for much longer. At some time or another, he will find out I'm a fake of some sort or another. This hurts.

The poet begins his second piece. I glance across the room and the Negroni girl is standing up. She excuses herself and edges her way towards the exit, which, fortunately for her, is on her side of the room. She can slip out easily. Me, on the other hand, I'm on the other side. How on earth am I going to get out of this place without having to walk right down in front of the poet who is rapping about how his mob have never been listened to?

I skirt around legs and tables of drinks. The local beatniks are giving me death stares as I disturb their poetry appreciation. I'm trying to act like I have some pressing biological function that demands my exit, and that I'm not some right-wing conservative phoney art lover who can't bear to be in the presence of an Indigenous man holding court and speaking truths.

I head down to the bar area and she's not there. I go over to the windows to see if I can spot her in the street. Can't see her. But then I can't see directly below as there is an awning that juts out over the pavement. I head down the stairs and walk nonchalantly out onto the street. I'm acting again, playing a part. I look to the left and there she is outside the twenty-four-hour gym. She is talking to a man in a hi-vis vest and work boots. There is a red Holden ute pulled up beside him on the side of the road and the passenger-side door is open. Through the rear cabin window of the ute, I see a bald head on the driver's side. I turn right and walk away until I get to the barber shop on the corner. I stand in the door recess, face the street and pull a pack of cigarettes out of my top pocket. I scan to my left again. They are still talking. I light up a cigarette.

Since I started freelance surveillance work, cigarettes have become a valuable tool of the trade. Bloody expensive, though, and I don't think I can claim them as a tax deduction. I imagine being audited. 'I hadn't smoked for ten years and took them up purely for the job. You know, smoking can get people talking to you. A lot of my subjects smoke, and if I do also, I can join them outside workplaces, in alleyways or on rooftops, and find out all sorts of stuff that otherwise would never be spoken about to a perfect stranger. Being a smoker these days is like being in some clandestine club, where members feel an affiliation that only comes from being shunned and pilloried and judged as weak by the mainstream. And when you're in that club, you trust each other and you talk about shit that you'd never tell a non-smoker. That's why I have to buy cigarettes to do my job. That's why I've put them down as a legitimate work expense.'

The tax inspector, or whatever job title they have, would cross it out with a red pen while giving me that special look that non-smokers give smokers.

My target and the bloke who's dressed like a road worker are still talking. Though it looks like it's getting a bit heated. I see her take a step back and point towards The Entrance. Perhaps she lives there. Their words are not discernible, but the volume, and the rhythm, and the tone, are easily heard as a disagreement. I continue my act as a mere smoker with no interest in their goings on. The man pulls his hand out of his navy blue King Gee work pants. He is holding something in his fist. He offers it to the girl. She waves her hands in front of her in rejection. He steps forward and leans forward, he growls in her ear. He pushes whatever he is holding into her stomach. She pushes into his chest, which only serves to push herself back, and she ends up against the dark grey wall of the gym.

Of course I'm thinking drugs. Cocaine, for sure. Cocaine is in.

The man on the street looks towards me. I edge back a bit into the door recess. If he saw anything, it would only be my profile and some smoke.

He is obviously confident that no one is watching, or cares, and yells at the girl, 'Fuckin' do it, OK?'

I step right back out of sight.

I hear a car door slam, and the ute revs up. I lean out and see the girl still standing against the wall. She is holding something in two hands at her stomach. The tyres squeal and the ute fishtails away up the street towards The Entrance. The girl hasn't moved.

I wait. I stub out my half finished cigarette and light up a fresh one. I'm acting again. I edge out a bit onto the pavement. I'm just a smoker, not concerned about a man yelling at a woman and a car spinning its wheels. It's all just par for the course, says my body language. I'm looking around at the night sky, looking across the street at the Obsidian Tambourine, where tomorrow I'll be watching Seamus make coffees while I pretend to write a short story.

I'm looking everywhere but at the girl, who I assume is now in possession of a quantity of cocaine in a clip-lock plastic bag.

I sense her. She is getting her shit together. She is deciding whether or not to go back up to the bar and get another Negroni, and wondering whether or not that will soothe her frayed nerves. Tossing up whether of not to go and listen to some more poetry. Thinking how she could maybe begin to move some of this contraband thrust upon her without consent. Surely, the poetry crowd hoover up coke like there's no tomorrow. She would know.

I step out into the middle of the pavement. Face south. My back towards her. Waiting, acting.

'Hey, mate, have you got a spare fag?'

Well, she's not going straight back into the Savoy. I turn around, put my cigarette into my mouth, and retrieve the smokes and lighter out of my top pocket.

She accepts my tools of the trade – see, Mr Tax Inspector – and lights up. 'Thanks,' she says. Now she will talk.

I say nothing and wait. I half expect her to be trembling or teary considering the angry confrontation she just endured. But she seems calm and collected.

'You going back up?' she asks.

'Nah. Had enough of poetry tonight. What about you?'

'I like spoken word poetry, but be fucked if I'm gunna pay another $15 for a drink.'

'I know what you mean.' I suck hard on my cigarette and blow the smoke up towards the windows of the bar.

'Wanna go and have a drink at the pub?'

'Why not?' says me.

I spent three days with Matilda. She'd been given an ounce of 'goey' to sell. It had been pre-packaged into 'eight balls'. I was wrong about it being cocaine. Appears that dirty old speed still has currency in the newly gentrified suburb of Long Jetty. And, to top it all off, Matilda doesn't know Seamus from a bar of soap.

Today, I'm coming down in my low-rent cabin down by the lake. I have to contact my employer, let them know why I haven't reported for three days. I make up some bullshit about my computer crashing and how I took notes by hand and have just caught up with all the typing and encryption. Looks like I'm a fiction writer after all. With the state my mind is in at the moment, I don't care how lame it sounds.

Needing coffee and fresh air, I head to the Obsidian Tambourine.

Seamus pops his head out over the espresso machine as I make my order. He asks if I want to go to the beach for a swim after he finishes work. It's bit of a shock, him being so forward.

'Why not?' I say.

I open up my laptop and start to write a short story. I have to have something to show Seamus. After three days of sex and speed and alcohol with Matilda, I think about writing some grunge lit. I could become the Charles Bukowski of Long Jetty. Punch out a couple of street psalms at the next poetry slam.

I type:

Ralph gave his girlfriend a merkin for Valentine's Day. She was not impressed and left him for a week. When she returned, he was lying on the floor of the bathroom, head shaved, clothes covered in mud, and smelling like the tip.
'What has happened?' she asked.
'Bush week,' he replied.

Seamus comes over with my coffee. He glances at the words on the screen.

'It's crap,' I say and backspace it all off the page.

'Want to swim across Toowoon Bay?' he asks.

'Why not?'

Why not? It's a rhetorical question. Another one. A persuasive rhetorical question to oneself. Why not get yourself into all sorts of trouble and strife, you weak person, you.

I think of Matilda. I don't expect I'll be seeing her for a while.

She wanted to go on. 'There's plenty of goey left,' she said. 'Go and get a bottle of gin.'

I asked what she was going to do when Gino came for the money.

'Fuck him,' she said.

Fuck him, I thought. That could mean several things. None of them good. So I went and bought a bottle of gin and I dropped it back to her place. I gave her fifty bucks as well and told her I had to go.

She grabbed my cock and asked, 'What about this then?'

'I have to go,' I repeated and walked away. I looked back as I closed the front gate and saw her swipe aside her messy hair to take a swig of the gin.

The coffee brings on a serious sweat. At some stage, I will have to sleep. I'll do it after the swim with Seamus. It's another hour until he knocks off. Talk about bush week, my head is scrubby and dry, a tinderbox, and bushfire season is starting earlier and earlier every year.

I start another story:

Sally slips between the sheets. She is nervous. It is Wednesday night. Her and husband Ralph have made an agreement about that night in the middle of the week. Hump Night they call it. She's not nervous about the routine sex with Ralph, it's the pubic hair down below. It's growing faster than expected, it's thick and black and prickly, it's ugly. It could upset Ralph, that's the problem.

He feels her stubble and makes a noise. A quiet, 'Ooh.'

'Sorry,' she says. 'Minnie is away on holidays. You know she's the only one who doesn't hurt.'

'It's OK,' he says. 'I don't mind.' Ralph starts again. This time in the know.

'You don't have to lick me there if you don't want,' Sally advises.

He doesn't lick her down there. He will hold off, wait until Minnie comes back and performs her Brazilian magic.

After sex, Sally says, 'That was nice.'

'Yes, it was.'

'Minnie's back next Monday. I see her on Tuesday after work.'

'You don't have to have do it. Maybe you could let it go for a while. It would save money. And I hear that bush is back in.' Ralph pokes Sally in her side.

They laugh.

'We'll see. Maybe I'll just get a bikini line done.'

'Whatever you want, Darl.'

They kiss and Ralph turns over and sleeps.

Sally can't sleep.

I stop there. I can't go further with this. This man/woman business is too tricky. A minefield. A PC minefield, to be precise. Critics would point out how Sally has been represented as weak and a sexual object. And the author is clearly white and straight and male. Clearly a misogynist.

Maybe I am a misogynist. Subconsciously marinated in toxic masculinity and incubated in the ovens of patriarchy and privilege to become the lowest form of dominant life on this planet. Bush week is over. The message is loud and clear. I'm a dinosaur watching the comet approaching. I'm a drunk at the bar on the *Titanic*. I'm a hedge fund manager on Wall Street in 2007. It's the end of days.

I remind myself how self-loathing is a natural part of coming down after an amphetamine binge. I forgive myself.

I type 'bush week' into Google. I get the history. Country folk invited to come and stay with city folk for a week in 1920. Bush week. That's a hundred or so years ago.

Did the country folk cause trouble? Or did they sit around and do nothing? Nowadays, country people come to the city for other reasons, not to improve rural-urban relations as was the hope in 1920.

Perhaps I can write a dystopian story. There's a market for them, apparently. The new de rigueur genre. Oh yes, I'm the great pretender. A genre writer. Why not?

I type:

The government calls a state of emergency. Any persons west of the Divide are to be evacuated from their homes and brought to the coast. There will be a one-off payment to any individual or family who agrees to take in a billet.

The emergency is climate change. It sneaked up faster than the lazy electorate and the growth-addicted governments ever imagined. Now, people are dying. Some areas, like the outback, have become totally uninhabitable. So have the low-lying coral islands, swamped. The sea rising fast and furious.

I stop again. That cliché did it – fast and furious. I do know a few things about fiction writing, and I know of the disdain for clichés.

I give up on the story writing. It's real life that ought to be my priority. The speed is still in my system. What am I doing? Now, that should be my focus. It's so easy to distract oneself. Especially when that self is a damaged and lost and neglected little self. And what about Seamus? I only see him as a good person. His backstory is a relic from some past life he was born into. He's done his time. Why can't he be left alone? Are the recidivism rates such that no ex-con can ever walk free? How long will they want me to spy on the fellow? I call him a fellow. I can't for a moment consider myself any better than Seamus. If anything, I judge him to be a better man than I.

People come and go from the Obsidian Tambourine. I watch them over the lid of my laptop. Seamus brings me another coffee, compliments of the house. It triggers off the sweating again. This time I smell it, the metabolites of ethanol, amphetamine and Matilda. Another wave of self-loathing hits hard. A swim will do me good.

Seamus is awkward on land, but he glides through water like a cutter. He's up ahead, setting the pace. I'm slapping away in short spurts trying to keep up. I can't go for long, I run out of breath and have to stop and tread water for a while. Seamus swims without pause and is pulling further away. I vow to stop smoking. Seamus reaches the end of the bay and turns back. We meet. He stops and asks if I'm OK. I tell him I'm heading into shore and will walk back and meet him on the beach where we placed our towels.

We sit for a while on the beach. Usually by this time of afternoon at this time of year, a nor'-easter will be blowing. Today it's still. The swim has helped somewhat with my coming down. I will be able to sleep tonight. I'm yearning for some sanity, some normality. But I don't know what that is. I have been transient for the last ten years; living in cabins, spying on adulterers and insurance cheats, eating poorly and oscillating from abstinence to binge. Something has to change. I've said this to myself before. This time, I'm thinking, I have to do it – I'm slowly killing myself.

Seamus starts to talk. 'I originally come from Freemantle. Have you ever been there?'

'Once, when I was a kid. My father took me there when he was on a business trip. I think I was about eleven. I'd never been on a plane before and my mother thought it would be good for me and my father to do something together. It didn't work out, though. We arrived and he got pissed in the pub we were staying at. The next morning he was grumpy, which wasn't unusual, he was always grumpy, around us family anyway, and he put me on an airport shuttle to Perth and I flew back to Sydney.'

'Was it the Federal Hotel? My father drank there.'

'No idea. My memory of that trip is very vague. I think I was in a constant state of anxiety when alone with my dad.'

'I know what you mean. My father claimed he was from a long line of Irish independence freedom fighters. But really, he was just a criminal. A self-appointed tough guy. So tough, in fact, that he bullied me into doing his dirty work for him while he held court at the Federal. I ended up doing six years for that. But you know that, don't you?'

A shot of adrenalin kicks in. So much for coming down after three days on speed. I try to read Seamus's face, wondering if he is going to attack. His face says nothing. He looks at me, trying to judge my reaction, I suspect. I suspect he sees my fear. I look down at the sand.

'It's OK,' he said. 'I have nothing to hide. You can spy all you want. Tell them everything. We all have to make a living. But we can't be friends. I wanted to tell you the other night at the Savoy, but it wasn't the right place. That's why I invited you for the swim today.' Seamus stands up and wraps his towel around his waist.

'I'm sorry, Seamus,' I say.

'Don't be sorry. Just don't try to be mates. Do what you have to and leave me be. When I got out of jail, I came over here from Perth. I'm never going back, and I'm never going back to jail.' He picks up his clothes as though he is about to leave. But he just stands there and looks out at the ocean. The nor'-easter starts up.

I'm sitting there waiting for him to go, feeling sick on the stomach thinking about all the lies I have told. I feel like the lowest form of life on earth. I have to leave this line of work. Seamus stands there not moving. Is he waiting for me to leave? If only the sand would swallow me up and end this most uncomfortable moment. I think about how all along Seamus was reluctant to engage, how he softly softly fobbed me off when I tried to be friendly by telling him about my bullshit writing career. It appears I can't read people at all. I can digitally record their movements and break into their homes and phones and computers, but I don't know people at all. I don't even know myself.

I stand up and pick up my stuff. 'I'm sorry, Seamus,' I say. 'I'm going home to quit my job. You won't ever see me again. I wish you all the best.'

He turns and looks at me. 'You know, that's probably a good idea. Because it will only be a matter of time before the other mob who are keeping an eye on me work out that you aren't a short story writer at all. And they don't play by the same rules that I imagine you are supposed to. Then you'd really get to know what bush week is. Best you get a long way away from me.'

Seamus walks off. And as his words sink into my thick skull, a second surge of adrenalin swamps the last remaining threads of my composure. I slump down onto the sand and drown in panic.

Once a nor'-easter starts, it won't let up. It will uproot umbrellas and whip up sand into the faces of toddlers, it will send all but the lifeguards home. It might ease overnight. But it will be back, and it will bring in bluebottles and cuttlefish bones. It's there to remind us that nothing is perfect, not even summer. Especially summer.

My shoulders are crusted with salt and my head is full of escape plans as I walk up to my cabin. I see Matilda sitting on my doorstep, head down and muttering to herself. I stop. She hasn't noticed me. I could turn around and leave quietly, but where would I go?

'Hey, what's up?' I say.

Startled, she snaps her head up. Her mane of ringlets flops back to reveal a smudged up reddened face. 'Can we go inside? Gino is around, he's looking for me. He'll kill me if he finds me.'

We go inside. I can smell the gin on Matilda. She is walking around in circles with her hands in her hair and muttering nonsense. She needs $3,000 for Gino. It appears that she and I consumed about half of that amount and that she has somehow lost the other half. I stand in her path and she crashes into me. I hold her to my chest and tell her everything will be OK and that I can get the money, no problems. She starts to sob. I take her into the bedroom and sit her down on the bed. I tell her she needs sleep. She nods and kicks off her sandals and lies down. I pull a sheet up over her. I close the Venetian blind. I leave her be.

Memories of Long Jetty bring mixed emotions. It was where I hit my last rock bottom – which, though a horrible and bad thing, was an inevitable eventuality, thus I now see how good it was for me. It was where I betrayed a tall and distant man who woke me up from a decade of restlessness and purposelessness. It was where I left $3,000 cash on a bed in a cabin with a note to a girl. I explained how there was a month's rent paid in advance on the cabin. 'Have it,' I wrote.

Ironically, the bank record of my unusually large withdrawal at The Entrance branch of the Westpac bank was picked up by a public servant at the Bondi Centrelink. Having no valid reason for the withdrawal, I was informed that I would have to wait three months before I would get Newstart. Desperate, I took on a cash-in-hand dish pig job at a café called the Salty Human Bean. Six days a week, I walk along the coast from the room I rent in Bronte to the café in Coogee. After work, I either swim laps in the ocean pool at Clovelly or I duck over to Gordon's Bay and dive into the ocean.

A few weeks ago, the boss starting training me to operate the espresso machine. I get the occasional stint when the chief barista ducks out the back for a piss and a smoke. And as I make the coffees, I think of Seamus and Matilda, and with a warmth that is only just returning to my soul, I wish them well.

Markets

20 January 2019

A monk in saffron robes wanders the Sunday market. He has a shaven head and carries a small dillybag. He is looking over some trinkets on a trestle table.

People look at him and wonder what on earth a monk is doing in a place like this.

The monk finds what he is looking for.

Nothing.

Milton Rowe

There he is again, down in the channel, water up to his thighs. He watches the carefully balanced pencil float drifting seaward with the tide, the onshore breeze in his face.

A couple, walking on the bridge above, stop. They see a school of mullet swimming close to the man but over to his left. 'Woohoo,' one of them calls out.

The man looks up.

'They're over there,' the woman calls and points.

'Big ones,' calls the man.

The fisherman waves in acknowledgement and continues fishing where he is.

The couple watch for a while and move off. 'We were only trying to help,' says one to the other.

The float disappears, he strikes and hooks onto a fish that bends his rod almost in a circle.

A man on the shore, watching and smoking, says to himself, 'Pound for pound, niggers are the best fighting fish around.'

The fish ends up in the keeper net with another one caught earlier. The net is tied to the strap on his wading bag. Later, he will be at the fish cleaning table next to the boat ramp, dispatching, scaling, gutting and beheading. The pelicans will gather around, each long beak centred on the man with the fish, anticipating the moments when he will fling them some morsels.

When the flathead are on, the man can be observed in the channel, not near the bridge, but further down towards the ocean. He has a white bucket with a battery-operated aerator attached. It keeps the poddy mullet that he trapped earlier alive and flicking. The man carefully lip-hooks the live bait and casts gently into the run-out tide. He watches his float and strikes a few seconds after it disappears below the surface.

People often have something to say to the man after he has finished fishing and is packing his gear into the car. They notice the fish in the green keeper net. Some share their misinformation about the sex changing ability of flathead.

Though he knows better, he simply responds, 'Is that so?' or 'Yes, I've heard that.'

The smoking man, the one who sees everything in this neck of the woods, looks at the catch and says, 'Nice lizards. Best eating fish if you ask me.'

The fisherman only ever takes what he can eat. He never fishes for mere sport. As he gets older, and one would guess him to be in his mid-thirties, the man is finding it harder and harder to kill these beautiful animals. One day, he thinks, he won't be able to fish any more.

On the white bucket, and on the red wading bag, handwritten in block letters with a permanent marker, is the name Milton Rowe, and underneath, a mobile phone number.

There it is, always in ripped jeans, all that visible thigh and yet no clearly discernible gender. The shoppers watch and avoid. He, or she, or whatever this may be, has meat, Mitchum deodorant and make-up removal pads in their red plastic Coles basket.

'It has to shop,' says the smoking man to the exasperated locals, who wonder whatever is the world coming to.

There she is again, up on the dance floor, skirt swishing around her thighs. With eyes closed, arms up in the air, the music washes through her, moving her body in rhythmic waves. The lights change colour and reflect off her copper lamé top.

A couple sitting at a table near the bar watch her dance. They have to lean in and talk directly into each other's ears to be heard.

She says, 'I think you fancy her.'

He says, 'You're kidding, she's not my type. Too muscly.'

She says, 'Looks like a slut to me.'

They drink their bourbons, they never dance. They go to restaurants, and to the movies and occasionally to barbecues at other people's places. Their friends are getting married, some are having kids. These two are biding time until the day they'll split up. Then they will be free to admit to themselves, and to divulge to others, all the things they hated about each other, intimate personal details included.

The nightclub patrons often ask the bar staff about the girl who dances alone. Her name is Millie, and yes, she always dances alone. The bar staff like Millie. She's not like most. She is polite and always leaves a tip in the jar on the bar. She has never had to be refused service. Her dancing is a joy to watch. She leaves at midnight, before the rowdiness.

Millie dances for two songs and returns to her table. She takes a sip of her drink. A man, chest out and confident, approaches Millie and asks for a dance. He – like all others, both men and women, who have asked before – is unsuccessful. He returns to his mates at the bar. They laugh at him. One mate punches his upper arm. Millie returns to the dance floor.

The man she rejected lifts up his arms, palms to the sky, questioning the universe.

The mate who punched him whispers in his ear, 'Carpet muncher.'

Another man, alone and in the corner, watches all this and spies Millie's handbag on the table.

Millie dances, lost in the music. The watcher edges over to her table. He opens the handbag and finds her purse. Inside is a driver's licence. There's a photo of a man. He sees Millie in the face on the licence. Name: Milton Rowe. He sees the address, a street he knows of in Long Jetty. He commits it to mind and goes outside to the smoking area.

Out there, the smoking man who sees all says to the watcher, 'Things aren't always what they seem, eh?'

Milton Rowe is leaving the area. There is no chance the bond will be refunded with all that offensive red graffiti over the walls that face the street. It's head north time, again. Wallis Lake and Boomerang Beach look promising for fishing. The shopping complex at Forster is large enough for anonymity. And Millie's dancing will be restricted to the lounge room at home, curtains drawn.

Bring a Plate

29 April 2019

Not sure what to take to the federal election party you've been invited to on 18 May?

These might work:

Mini pork barrels – great treat for those in marginal seats.

Don chips – an all-time favourite to keep the bastards honest.

Some greens – you know they're good for you.

Raw onions – popular in Warringah.

Cold democracy sausage – pork, lamb, beef, chicken, kangaroo and tofu all minced together with so much garlic and chili you won't hav ea clue what your eating.

Free trade gluten-free locovarian vegan nibblies – don't worry if no one eats them, the chooks might give 'em a shot the next morning.

Halal raspberry tart – available exclusively from the fish and chip shop in Ipswich, just ask for Pauline.

Bowl of mixed nuts – pick up some at Fraser Anning's next rally.

Mashed potato head – skin Dutton, boil Dutton, mash Dutton, hopefully this dish will be gone by seven p.m. AEST election night.

Cheese and frackers – they're a gas, gas, gas, all proceeds go to buying back puddle water from the Cayman Islands.

Pigs in blankets – Michaelia Cash is screaming about these.

Little boys – favourites of Family First and the Christian Democrats.

Chicken wings – left and right wings on separate plates please.

Frankingfurters – absolutely super!

Has Anybody Ever Told You

One way you can catch flathead is by flicking a soft plastic lure right in front of their flat heads. They mistake the oscillating plastisol for the real thing. The colour and size of the lure doesn't seem so important; it's the motion and placement that fools. I wonder, when a flathead is being reeled in, if it asks the lure, 'Has anybody ever told you you look like a poddy mullet?'

I get mistaken all the time for other people. For a while, it really worried me. I began to think, I must have a soft plastic head. After such cases of mistaken identity, I'd look at myself in the mirror to make sure that some rogue plastic surgeon hadn't snuck into my bedroom overnight and used me as a guinea pig to create a Shirley Bassey face on my unsuspecting white male head.

Yes, once I was asked, 'Has anybody ever told you, you look like Shirley Bassey?' Admittedly, this person was intoxicated, and the lighting was poor, and, I had just sung 'History Repeating' at the Long Jetty Hotel Karaoke Competition. But, Shirley Bassey? Though she's a great singer and very likely a nice person, I didn't take it as a compliment.

Despite obviously looking the part, I didn't win at karaoke that night. I went home and looked in the mirror. I tried to find Shirley in my face. And I tried to find Winston Churchill, as I have been likened to him more than once. Then I tried to find Jack Thompson, Jack Nicholson, Bill Shorten, Bill Cosby, Neil Young, Neil from the Young Ones, Brad Pitt, the Dalai Lama, Timomatic, Richard Nixon, Richard Attenborough, Albert Einstein, the professor from the Back to the Future trilogy, and the guy who used to sell things on the shopping channel by chucking in a set of steak knives. I couldn't find any resemblances. What were people seeing? I could only see me, yet others were seeing something. And not only that, by starting with 'Has any-body ever told you…' they were obviously assuming that they were not alone in making the same connection.

Should I answer, 'Oh yeah, everyone tells me I look like (insert name of whoever they imagined in my face)'? It might make them feel less stupid for asking such a stupid question.

I went to my computer and found Shirley and the Propeller Heads on Youtube. I laughed, both at my remembrance of how badly I had actually sung that night, and at how on earth someone could have thought I looked anything like this Welsh-born Dame famous for her James Bond theme songs and her desire to spend a little time with hand-some spendthrifts. They must have been taking the piss. But no, this sort of thing happened all the time. I was getting worried. Worse, I was getting seriously self-conscious.

During the peak of my 'has anybody ever told you' period, I started disguising myself when I went out in public. I tried hiding under broad-rimmed hats and dark sunglasses only to be asked, 'Has anybody ever told you you look like one of them spies from *Spy versus Spy*?' Bloody hell! So I added a fake moustache, only to be outed as the villain from *V for Vendetta*. This mistaken identity business was increasing in fre-quency and outrageousness. In utter desperation, I went to the local St Vincent's op shop and got myself a whole kit of middle-aged women's clothing and a wig. It was a waste of twenty-two dollars.

'Has anybody ever told you you look like Mrs Doubtfire?' Then, I got Margaret Thatcher. Next, Nancy Reagan.

Finally, the straw that broke my back happened when this kid in Kmart pointed at me and said to his mum, 'I thought Aunty Flo was dead.'

Thus, my period as a recluse began. Don't worry, it wasn't too long. My apartment quickly filled up with polystyrene boxes, courtesy of Woolworths' easy-peasy internet shopping services. Eventually, it got so cluttered in my house I had to go outside to get some proper circu-lation going in my legs. I'd forgotten how nice the sun could feel and how efficiently a breeze could refresh. I could never be a hermit. On the upside, during my two months of indoor isolation, I found an online community of people who were constantly told they looked like other people. Sheila, from Indianapolis, who I remain in contact with to this day, helped me to see that being likened to other people is not an affliction at all. It's a gift, she wrote. Coincidentally, she also likes fishing as much as I do. She casts lures into the Eagle Creek Reservoir for large-mouth bass, crappies and catfish. She says that though there is joy in people seeing someone else in you, sometimes it is nice to have a break, and people leave you alone while you're flicking lures. She's right.

Thanks to Sheila, and others in the group, now when I get asked the 'has anybody ever told you' question, I smile and answer, 'Yes. I get told that all the time,' even when they name some totally random person that I've never been likened to before. People love it when they are told they are not on their Pat Malone in this regard. After I say yes, I ask if they have ever been likened to anyone else. Invariably, they scrunch up their faces and try to recall if it has ever happened to them. Sometimes, someone will remember a past case of likeness recognition and I say, 'Oh yeah. I can see that.' But mostly they reply, 'No, I don't think so.' Then I joke with them and tell them they look like Batman, or Batwoman, depending on what gender I see in them.

One day, I was flicking some plastisol lures in the channel down at Picnic Point. I wasn't having any luck. I don't know if the flathead were there or not, or whether their stomachs were full of real poddy mullet – just one of the mysteries of fishing. And I have come to the realisation that mysteries are what makes life interesting, and also what makes me want to live for a long long time. I have this notion that if I live long enough, a lot of mysteries will be solved, and better still, new mysteries will become evident. In regard to my face, I have resigned myself to accept that I may never know why people see other faces in it. I'm getting to know myself better, and to be grateful for what I call my universal face. And this day down at the channel, which I now recount, will illustrate to some extent what I mean.

A group of people were at the electric barbecues while I fished. I knew exactly what was going on. It was a day activity for a small group of people with disabilities; you see it more and more now since the government funded this sort of thing. It's great, I reckon. No more hiding away of the people we have no idea of how to deal with.

The workers were obvious. They were alternating between helping at the barbecue, smoking, and talking on their mobile phones. The participants, which I believe is the correct terminology for recipients of NDIS funding, were engaged in all sorts of activity. Some helped with the browning of onions, the flipping of burger patties, and the margarining of bread rolls. Others wandered around looking at the lake and the trees, or simply looking at the ground. One young girl with Down syndrome stood on the shore and watched me fishing.

My left foot was getting wet and cold from a leak in my waders. My attempts to fix this troublesome issue with Shoe Goo had failed once again. I waded back into shore – no fish and numb toes. The young girl was still watching me. I picked up my backpack and she came over.

'You look like my dad,' she said. She didn't preempt with the standard, 'Has anybody ever told you…' which was a lovely surprise.

Caught off guard somewhat, I put my rod and bag down on the ground and opened my arms towards the girl. She came straight over and we hugged. Unforgettable.

One of the support workers noticed what was going on and came over. I thought, this could be tricky.

But all the worker said was, 'How you doing, buddy?'

They didn't see anyone else in my face. It was one of those win-win situations. An uplifting hug and a simple uncomplicated greeting, both from total strangers. I had let go of my stuff and the world responded.

Tell me, who do you think I look like?

Want a Gig?
28 June 2019

While the media focuses on stagnant wage growth, many workers' incomes are shrinking. Their companies have developed smartphone apps which enable their services to be delivered 24/7. Scheduled hours with an hourly rate are a thing of the past, or, if not totally extinct, they are critically endangered, rapidly disappearing.

To earn, the worker must make themselves available on the app and be able to drop everything and get to the workplace, likely a computer, or get to the customer and start work within a tight time limit designated by the company. And you will need to respond quickly to the app on the smartphone, or someone else, a work colleague whom you've never met, will snap up the work.

You'll get paid by the minute or the piece. It will be a minimum casual rate, with no on-call allowance, no penalty rates and no questions welcomed. You will be persuaded to believe that this great new technical innovation will be beneficial for everyone involved. Most workers will know upfront that this company-speak is bullshit. Those initially fooled by the hyped-up propaganda will soon learn the truth as their income shrinks and their work becomes sporadic and thinly spread over every hour of every day.

It's the gig economy. We didn't ask for it, but we got it because the company gets what the company wants. And nothing's as precious as increased profits.

Some of Us

After the acknowledgement to country, we were instructed about the emergency exits and the toilets. The Hawaiian-shirted, bearded man, the MC we assumed, made jokes about the weather and the general craziness of the world in these times. Then he initiated a slow clap which predictably increased in frequency. Some of us cringed, others wholeheartedly joined in. There was whooping and hollering and the stamping of feet.

Then she came out. And if you thought we were sufficiently revved up by the MC, you were wrong. The clapping and hooting ramped up to a whole new level – the crowd went wild, as they say.

She did a few laps around the stage, acknowledging the collective reception, and somehow, with eyes blinded by spotlight, she managed to find some individuals in the crowd and she acknowledged them personally. Some lucky soul down near the front got a thumbs up, and then someone else right up the back got blown a kiss. Then she put her hands to her chest and did half a bow to communicate how humbled she was by all this attention.

She centred herself on stage behind the microphone, lowered her gaze and breathed for a while. Like good children at the feet of the guru, we knew this was the signal to quieten down and get ready for our lessons. Most of us had paid good money for this opportunity, though some people had come for free. The local radio and newspaper had been giving away tickets for what was claimed to be the event of the year. One night only.

Some of us were not converts. We came along either out of curiosity, or we came so that if ever asked we could say, 'Yes, I have seen her in person.'

She started with this: 'It's not easy feeling unique in a world of seven point seven billion people. And worse than that, it's even harder to feel as though you belong.'

The crowd erupted. Some of us knew she started every show with the same lines. What came next was an hour and a half of short sharp platitudes, each one followed by fervent applause that would increase in duration and intensity until some of us started entering into trance-like states. Some of us even collapsed to the floor.

Who was she?

She was coloured. Proudly so.

She was a she. And though men and women were equal in all respects, she made it clear how men were wholly to blame for the woes of the world. Apparently, she told us, her wife felt the same.

She was a first nation person. Not from here but over there. She highlighted the evils of colonisation. She insisted we adopt the old ways. She wore a hijab. She was a Muslim. A lesbian Muslim.

She was, by virtue of all that she was, unimpeachable.

As would be revealed later on, she was a phoney, a total fake, a blue ribbon show pony. Her resume, her pedigree, her sincerity, was all bullshit. Some of us there that night, at the Long Jetty Town Hall, sensed as much. We saw her ambitious posturing. We smelt the ego, recognised the taste of her fashionable clichés, heard the obvious lies, and felt with a shiver her need for adoration. What was harder to understand was the mob's susceptibility. Somehow, she had tapped into, and feasted upon, the fear and ignorance of the masses.

There were, that night, some of us women in the know. Some of us gay people knew. And there were some of us blacks and browns and yellows in the know. Some of us first nation people knew she was a fraud. And though not free from the guilt born of the sins of past generations, some of us white colonials were also in the know.

Those in the know, who witnessed this parade as charade, stayed silent – at the time. The time was not yet ripe. So we placated our fury and disappointment with whispers and knowing glances to those others who we knew to be in the know.

The world did change. Slowly and steadily, mostly, but sometimes in spits and spurts. And sometimes with unimaginable, unpredictable and unprecedented events. And then, all of us, not just some, we watched the Youtube history of her highness on her town hall tour, and we laughed with impunity at the folly of it all.

Socialists Have Aspirations as Well
10 July 2019

Dear Prime Minister,

It's pretty clear that you and your side of politics believe that any form of taxation or welfare destroys people's aspirations. I speak for myself while suspecting I am not alone, especially since at the last federal election more people voted for Labor and the Greens than voted for your so called broad church coalition of neo/liberal/conservative/national parties.

I have lots of aspirations. One of them I can phrase in your very own faux fair dinkum ozzie parlance. It is: a fair go so we can all have a go. It sounds a lot like your mantra – a fair go for those who have a go – but it is quite different, and the type of society that would emanate from my philosophy would be quite different from the one you are currently legislating into existence.

If you're having trouble understanding the difference, let me use this horticultural analogy. One gardener, let's call him Bluey, sows a field of wild flower seeds. The other gardener, let's call her Cerise, does the same. Bluey likes to keep a tight rein on his gardening budget so he waits until the seeds sprout before he decides which plants will get water, mulch and fertiliser. Cerise has already fertilised and mulched the soil and she regularly waters the whole field.

It doesn't take long before some of the wild flowers in Bluey's patch sprout and grow tall and strong. Bluey gives them lots of water and all the fertiliser they need, he mulches around them and sings their praises. 'Why, look at this tall strong blue flower – it is clearly having a go. It deserves to be well looked after.'

After some time, Bluey's field contains a smattering of tall thriving blue flowers. 'Look how they reach for the sky, they will be an inspiration for all the other flowers who are not so tall or strong. Oh, what a good gardener am I.'

Cerise's garden has blue flowers as well, but they don't stand out like the ones in Bluey's garden because they are surrounded by a multicoloured blanket of floral delights. By feeding, watering and tending to the whole field, each variety of flower can thrive and blossom.

Not all flowers aspire to be the tallest.

Scott, I believe that the brand of aspiration you and your adherents claim that socially progressive political parties wish to destroy, is the aspiration that drives some people to become wealthy by winning at the brutal game of capitalism.

I don't aspire to be wealthy, but I do aspire. I aspire to live in a society that is well watered and fertilised, a society where every person is looked after so they can thrive in a multicoloured field of wild and unique humans.

Call me a socialist if you will. Yes, a small red flower, that for a long time now has been wrongly accused of being something that it is not. I am not a communist, I am not a soldier of class warfare. I am not envious of the rich and influential. I aspire for things other than money and power. I aspire for peace and equality and for our human society to tread a whole lot more lightly on the planet and all its life forms.

Scomo, you have been elected to serve all the peoples of Australia. Please understand that not all of us aspire to get ahead of the pack to be tall poppies in the corporate world that is destroying the planet with its dogged pursuit of growth and profits. Welfare and taxation are the water and fertiliser for a healthy society. Most of us would prefer to live in Cerise's garden and not Bluey's.

Fair dinkum,

Sean

Do Not Reply To This SMS

I make plans. Lots of them. Plans that I have no intention of ever carrying out. They remain inside my brain, electrochemical algorithms, beautiful and untainted by reality. Once you start to enact a plan, imperfections creep in and eventually everything fails.

Yesterday, a woman sat next to me on the bench from where I watch the sunset and make plans – like going to Western Australia one time to watch the sun set into the sea.

The woman asked if I was meditating.

I thought about it and replied, 'Yes.' I could tell she wanted more of a conversation.

She commented on the beauty. About how dark the hills looked, and how the glassy water mirrored the sky.

'Yes,' is all I said.

She bade me farewell and wished me a pleasant evening.

Her plan, whatever it may have been, was ruined. Ruined by me? No. It was ruined by the mere fact that she enacted her plan. It wouldn't have mattered what I said. I could have engaged in a lengthy and enjoyable conversation which led to a friendship. We might have even ended up lovers. And if that was her plan, she would have one day thought, 'Taking that leap and sitting down next to the man by the lake worked out exactly as planned.' But believe me, one day it would all come unstuck. Maybe soon, or maybe after years. The inevitable demise might be sudden and dramatic, or it might be gradual, a slide into oblivion barely noticeable. But it would all end. I know.

It was a Wednesday morning when Australia woke up to see the planes crashing into the World Trade Center (sic) towers. Breakfast television.

They ended up naming this unnameable event 9/11. For us, it was 12/9. Everything upside-down, inside-out, back to front. It was 2001. I make this point solely because this Wednesday was the day I entered into an agreement with a woman called Margaret. It lasted fifteen years, this arrangement. With hindsight, I can say that the first five years were great, the next five bearable, and the last five were pretty much a disgrace.

Towers fall. Relationships decay.

It was an unusual arrangement. We finalised it over dinner at the Bateau Bay pub. I remember she had steak and I had fish. While people were sipping beers and Chardonnays and watching the endless loops of the unspeakable acts of terror on the endless TV screens around the pub walls, Margaret and I planned an open de facto relationship. We agreed to commit to five-year blocks. We planned to buy a house and have our own bedrooms. And we did it. As per the plan, when we had sex, we did it in the third bedroom, doggy style, always. Margaret regularly went on cruises and had sex with other people. I rarely holidayed, but I did have a long-term affair with a married woman at my work. Margaret and I knew what was going on; it didn't matter as it was all set out in our arrangement. All part of the plan. We kept our dalliances outside of the home. We co-inhabited.

We were both thirty years of age when we met. Brian Alessandro introduced us at his turn-of-the-millennium New Year's party. I recall Margaret and myself sharing stories about our past relationships. There were some interesting parallels. And I remember neither of us could give two hoots about the Y2K bug. We dated, we were compatible, but after a few times in the sack, she knew, and I knew, that there were no fireworks going on in that department. It didn't matter. We wanted to be a couple. Being part of a couple, we felt, was so much easier and simpler than being single. We started nutting out the arrangement. We got what we planned.

Incidentally, we lost contact with Brian and his cocaine-snorting crew of beautiful people. Then one day out of the blue, perhaps five years after the party where we met, Margaret and I, after a swim at

Toowoon Bay, noticed Brian in the distance. Margaret went over to say hello. She knew him better than I. I watched them talking. Then a lady in an aqua-coloured polo shirt came over and spoke to Margaret. They talked for while and Brian wandered off. Then the care worker, that's what she was, led Brian back to a picnic shelter where a group of elderly people were having morning tea.

Margaret came back shocked. Brian had early-onset dementia. He didn't even recognise her.

'He's living in a nursing home, because there's nowhere else,' said Margaret.

'I wonder if it was all the drugs?'

'Well, if that's the case, there's a whole lot of his friends who should be in that nursing home to keep him company.'

'True,' I said. 'I reckon it's his name that's the problem.'

Margaret looked at me and knew a joke was coming. 'Go on,' she encouraged.

'It's pretty obvious really. Think about it. Brian: B, R, I, A, N. It's brain mixed up.'

She laughed. It eased her shock somewhat.

She liked my sense of humour, back then. Eventually, it drove her mad. Eventually, it was just one of many reasons that resulted in the dissolution of our arrangement. On our fifteenth anniversary at the Bateau Bay pub, she had steak and I had fish. And we ended it. Perfect bookends for a not so perfect relationship.

I suspect that the woman who asked me if I was meditating on the bench down by the lake will come back. Call it a hunch. She'll be back. My lack of interest will be bugging her. She is not used to men being like I was. She will want to know more about me. She suspects I'm single and will want to know why and how and who I have been with before. So I have a plan. I will tell her a story. I will tell her how my one and only long-term relationship ended for one reason. Not many reasons, as is the truth, but one reason only. A silly and trivial reason. It will be a true thing, this silly trivial reason, but it is not the sole reason. People like simple stories with clear cause and effect.

When this woman comes back to find out more about me. I will, unlike yesterday, give her all my attention. I will satisfy her curiosity. And the story I tell will ensure that she'll never come back and talk to me. I will have the sunsets all to myself, again.

Here is the story.

My relationship ended with Margaret due to a succession of text messages that I kept getting on my mobile phone which I rarely used and only possessed as a requirement of my work. They were automated texts from the Parents and Friends of Corpus Christi College in Perth, Western Australia. Obviously, someone made an error entering mobile phone numbers into the computer program that does all this automatic texting. The texts would inform of meeting times, changes to meeting times, changes to the usual meeting place (once, it was due to an asbestos scare), how to submit items for the agenda and other matters that now escape my memory. I would get these texts several times a week, usually on weekday evenings when Margaret and I were at home together living out our arrangement.

My phone was always this thing that I didn't want, but had to have. It never rang and I never got texts. Margaret was on her mobile phone all the time. Margaret was a lot more social and outgoing than me. I put this down to the fact that Margaret worked pretty much on her own as an accountant for a law firm. She worked behind a computer screen all day in an office space that was separate to the admin department and other parts of this busy firm that specialised in family law. Outside of work, Margaret needed social interaction. In my case, I worked all day with lots of people, face to face. I needed solitude after work. In terms of our arrangement, this worked fine. We had planned to have separate lives. When we were home together, Margaret's phone was dinging all the time with incoming texts.

One thing that Margaret and I did do together was television. In the early years, we watched live television and rented DVDs; by the end, it was all streaming. We watched all sorts of stuff, from foreign movies to cooking shows, from HBO television series to daily news and current affairs. In the beginning, we would have long discussions about the show we had just watched. We would each have a different slant on certain aspects of the characters or the plot or whatever. We liked those differences, we learned from each other. Whenever we sat down and watched together, Margaret's phone would go ding, ding, ding. She would deal with all the texts later, after our discussion, after we had gone to our separate bedrooms. I never once said anything about all those dings.

On 12 September 2011, the tenth anniversary of our open de facto relationship, we both, as per the arrangement, recommitted to another five years. It was a Monday night. We watched *Four Corners*, we ate grilled chops and steamed vegetables. We decided to stay at home and not go to the pub as we usually did each anniversary. We should have called it quits. We both knew that the arrangement had lost its lustre. We were just like a married couple and as we watched the story about Australia losing its bid to host the World Cup of Soccer, or football, as it supposedly should be called, we stupidly agreed to another five years.

'Shall we do another five, Margaret?' I tried to put on bit of an upper-class British accent.

'I guess so,' she replied.

'Don't sound so enthusiastic. You know this is your chance to bail out, no questions, fifty-fifty split, walk away, no hard feelings. You know, the arrangement?' I couldn't ever hold an accent and as I gave Margaret this opportunity to end our deal, my accent morphed from British to Scottish and then finally to Indian. I practically wobbled my head as I uttered 'arrangement'.

'I can't see a reason to end what we have. It's working well, don't you think?'

'I guess so,' I said.

After the *Four Corners* episode, with another five-year block verbally agreed to, we talked a bit about professional sport.

Margaret made a good point. 'I wonder how much Nicole Kidman got paid to tout that fucking "our island home" crap?' It was a good observation, a good question.

Margaret went to her bedroom to reply to the texts that came in as we watched telly and ate dinner. I knew she was planning her next cruise. I suspected the texts were from her partner in crime, Chelsea. She was Margaret's cruise buddy. I knew they got up to lots of drinking and partying with strangers. Chelsea would post stuff on Facebook, and Harriet Smyth, the married woman who wouldn't accept that I didn't want to continue our illicit affair, would show me and say, 'Your wife is a slut. You know that, don't you?'

'She's not my wife, she's my de facto. You know that.'

De facto: the best term I could use to describe Margaret. I couldn't say lover, or soulmate, and partner never felt right when I occasionally tested it out at the occasional social events that Margaret and I attended as a couple. 'This is Margaret, my partner,' I would say uncomfortably. In the end, I decided to introduce her simply as Margaret, and hold her hand or put my arm around her shoulder to intimate we were, to all intents and purpose, a couple. I only used de facto when pushed for a category.

That night when we so casually signed up for another five years, when Margaret went off into her bedroom to get all revved up about her next cruise with Chelsea, we didn't use the third bedroom. I'm pretty sure we had never missed having sex as part of our anniversary ritual. It would affirm a tacit understanding, not explicitly written into our arrangement, that we could and would have sex when either one of us was needing that kind of release.

Yes, I should have ended the relationship that night. It's easy to say with the wisdom of hindsight. At the time, though, it was the least confronting option. And if I want to get defensive, I can testify that the relationship was functioning. We never argued. We both did what we wanted within the framework of the arrangement. And the quick doggy-style fucks in the third bedroom, except for this ten-year anniversary night, hadn't decreased in frequency or intensity or outcome.

From that night on, things went downhill. We still watched television together, but the after-episode discussions became shorter and less enjoyable. I could tell Margaret was fake laughing at my jokes and foreign accents. And though I once found her observations and opinions insightful, they were now painfully predictable. We both knew what was going on; we could see it in the micro expressions we learnt about from watching the series *Lie to Me*. But we stuck to our arrangement. No yelling or raising of voices. No sarcastic jibes.

For the sake of the story, I will tell the woman when she comes back to the bench at sunset with her plan to break down my wall of indifference, that my phone first went ding during the fourth episode of season three of *Mad Men*. If that's not exactly true, it's close enough. I know, because during our after-episodes discussions it became clear that Margaret had a big crush on Don Draper. She couldn't stand me picking apart his character.

In self-defence – or was it retribution? – she claimed that it was obvious I was keen on Betty. 'And I thought you didn't like blondes,' she added.

I'm sure if you ask Margaret about the demise of our relationship, she would confer that things weren't great after the ten-year mark. She might even mention the tension that waxed and waned over the seven seasons of *Mad Men*. For some reason, this particular drama, set on the other side of the world in the previous millennium, had the capacity to arouse unsettling emotions in both her and myself. To our credit, we stuck to our arrangement and never yelled or raised our voices. But the cracks that were always there, if we were to be honest, were widening, and not so easy to ignore or smooth over. On some nights as we binged through the series, we wouldn't talk at all.

Ironically, episode four, season three is titled 'The Arrangements'. Partway through the episode, my phone went ding. It never went ding. Margaret looked at me. I could see the surprise in her face. I was surprised as well. And I could see irritation in her micro-expressions. We both looked back to the show. Betty Draper's father was dying, just like all things, just like our arrangement. The text would have to wait.

The episode finished.

'You got a text. Are you going to look at it?'

'Hang on,' I said, 'what did you think about that?' I pointed at the television.

'I think Betty is a bad actor. Now pick up your phone. I'm dying to know who texted you. You never get texts.'

'I think January Jones is a good actress, Peg.' Occasionally, I would call Margaret 'Peg'. More so since we'd been watching this show. She hated it. I called her Peg tonight because I was pissed off.

I was pissed off because she was irritated when my phone dinged during the show. Fair enough, I guess, since Margaret had in more recent times begun to turn her phone to silent during our nightly viewing. When the multiple texts do come in, as they inevitably do, her phone makes a little buzz on the coffee table as it vibrates in silent mode. That's irritating. Maybe, if she looked at me when it buzzed, she would see my micro-expressions of irritation. I was also pissed off that she wanted to know who texted me. I never asked who texted her.

'Don't call me Peg, OK?'

'Well, it's hard when *Mad Men* is mainly about Peggy. Did you see when she posted that card on the noticeboard that she signed off, Margaret Olsen?'

'Are you going to look at that text or not?'

I picked up the phone and opened the text. I read it out. It was the Parents and Friends of Corpus Christi College advising that next meeting would be in the gymnasium instead of the main hall.

'What?' she said.

'They must have my number by mistake.'

'Well, you should text them back and get them to take you off their list. Or else you'll need to put your phone on silent when we're watching TV.'

'I can't text back. It says at the end,' and I read it out, 'THIS IS AN AUTOMATED SMS – DO NOT REPLY.'

'Just do it anyway. How annoying. You don't want that happening all the time.'

'I don't know. It's kind of nice to be getting a text message for a change. Makes me feel popular.' It was a dig. I know that. It was passive aggressive. Not acceptable, but I did it. I informed Margaret that texting back would be pointless, that the text was generated by a computer program and any reply would go into some virtual never-never world.

'I know that,' she said. 'You could look them up and send an email.'

We went to our bedrooms.

I made no effort to get off the automated SMS system. And the texts started coming regularly.

We were only at season three. There was a lot to go – months actually. It was spring and Margaret joined a mixed tennis competition on Wednesday evenings. Combine that with her usual every second Thursday night book club, and the fact that we watched *Four Corners* every Monday night and how we never watched TV on the weekends, this only left Tuesdays and one Thursday a fortnight. We stuck at it and watched the transformation of Don Draper into a hippy, the ice cream induced ballooning of Betty Draper, and the blossoming of Peggy Olsen into a thoroughly modern working woman heading confidently into the halcyon feminist decade, the 1970s.

There has been a lot of discussion about the final episode of *Mad Men*. You can join the discussion on the internet. Margaret and I didn't say a thing. The series finished. We decided that we needed a break from all this television bingeing.

The P & F texts were still coming thick. There was a Christmas party scheduled for 2 December at Cicerello's at Fremantle. You could get tickets from Sue, apparently. I didn't know Sue, but I did know Gail. One day, and I never told Margaret about this, I emailed the P & F and asked them two questions. Firstly, why was the organisation called Parents and Friends rather than the more commonly used Parents and Citizens, and secondly, could a person with no connection to the school who lived in NSW become a member. Gail emailed me back.

It turned out Gail was the secretary. And she didn't think I was a crackpot, as I expected would be the case. She answered both questions with seriousness and common sense. Though, she did ask why on earth

I would want to become a member. I told her about the automated SMS messages I had been receiving. I told her how I looked up the school's website and that was how I got the P & F email address. I also told her that I planned to come to Perth soon to see a west coast sunset, which might have been triggered by Don Draper's move to LA, and figured, since I knew nobody in that part of the world, that I might rock up to the P and F and meet some locals. She thought it was a great idea, and we began a regular correspondence. She said I didn't have to join, but she'd keep me on the SMS database.

Confession: I planned to go Perth, but I knew I would never carry it out. It was to remain a plan, perfect in my mind. Never to be adulterated by cruel realities.

When I showed Margaret the text message with an invite to a Christmas party in Fremantle, she rolled her eyes and continued to unpack her groceries into the fridge. Eating arrangements were never stipulated in our open de facto relationship contract. In the beginning, we ate together and shared the cooking. In the end, we ate separately and had our own sections in the pantry and the fridge.

'You should go. Perth is amazing.'

'You know me. Home bod.'

'Sure,' she said.

She knew me and we had agreed from the start that we would never try to change each other. And we didn't. And you could say that was a good thing or not. I would still argue that it was a good thing, and it should be a thing that all couples agree upon. How many relationships do you see where one person tries to change the other? And what becomes of that? Never anything good, I observe. And I don't think if I tried to be more like Margaret – outgoing and adventurous, for example – that that would have saved our arrangement. I think in the end it simply ran its course. That the law of entropy applies to everything. The terms of our arrangement, as solid and foolproof as we initially thought, were not immune from whatever law of impermanence you might subscribe to.

So it wasn't simply the DO NOT REPLY text messages. They did piss Margaret off. And keeping them coming, and making jokes about them, and being my usual odd self, was no longer quirky and interesting for her. And I knew it, and I made sure that this no-longer-amusing part of me was right in her face. And she knew what was no-longer-of-interest to me about her. And she made sure that her oddness and eccentricities were right in my face as well. She made sure I overheard her conversations with Chelsea about their next cruise. She put her mobile on speaker and I could hear Chelsea getting all excited how on this Mediterranean cruise there would be less Aussies bogans and more sexy European men. I heard the term 'great lovers' being used several times.

I've never been jealous of Margaret being with other men. I think she may have been with women as well. None of that mattered. She was likely thinking of other people when we did our thing in the third bedroom. I know I was. I had planned lots of interludes with other women that never happened. But when behind Margaret, as per our arrangement, I could act out those plans in my mind. Margaret was like my virtual reality interface. The night when she had a dig about how I supposedly didn't like blondes, she became Betty Draper.

By now, Margaret's dalliances on cruises and who knows where else, had become a bore to me. When I was younger, I thought open relationships were modern and progressive. Now I see them as immature and superficial.

As it all came tumbling down in that final year, we never raised a voice or yelled. But it was over, and by the time we had finished with *Mad Men*, we both knew it was over, and we both knew it was nine months before our fifteenth anniversary. Nine months before we could agree not to sign up for another five years.

But when that woman comes back to my bench by the lake, I will tell her, when she asks, that I am single all because of an automated text message I received by mistake in the spring of 2015.

Margaret and I never had children. That was part of the arrangement. We not only agreed on the matter of overpopulation, we also both knew that we were damaged goods as a result of poor parenting, and thus not good parenting material ourselves. Would kids have made a difference? Could they have bought us closer together? Or could having kids have had us hating each other? Margaret and I never hated each other.

When we did split, having no kids made it less complicated. The biggest decision was who got which house. There was the house in Forresters Beach which we lived in, and then there was our investment property in Long Jetty. Initially, I was a bit against the whole negative gearing thingamajig. I work in welfare and housing affordability is a huge issue. But I went along with the plan to buy a house and rent it out. Margaret made a good case for it. When we split, I agreed to take the rental property, even though it was run-down and worth less on the open market. I was glad to get more of sea breeze and be close to the lake which is really a lagoon. Margaret clearly wanted our house and, to her credit, she offered to pay me out for the valuation difference. It wasn't necessary. I told her it was good how we could be amicable and go our ways with no serious regrets or animosity.

We remained civil to the end.

About a month before our fifteenth anniversary, the tenants at Long Jetty moved out.

'I don't think we should get new tenants just yet,' said Margaret.

'I agree.'

We both knew what was coming. We'd taken up television again, and said nothing more about the rental property and went and watched episode six, season three of *Vikings*. Margaret rooting for Ragna, me for Lagatha.

I have all sorts of plans for my Long Jetty house. A deck out the back would be nice, so would a paint job. I can see it in my mind, and that is better than all the angst and anxiety that would result from actually doing it.

Margaret and I are still friends. Friends with no benefits. She laughs again at my jokes. I am interested in her next cruise holiday.

'So what are you watching on telly lately?' I asked her one day when she delivered what she felt was a fair share of our collection of old photos.

'I'm getting into Nordic noir. Have you watched any of that?'

'Yeah! I'm loving *The Bridge*. I'm halfway through season three.'

'How good is it. Don't you just love Saga?'

'I do, actually. She reminds me of you in some ways.'

I made Margaret a plunger coffee and myself a pot of tea. We sat and talked. I pointed out the back door to where a deck could be built. We both knew it would never happen.

Later, when I went through my share of the photos, I figured out that there were no prints that would date after about 2006. The hard-copy images of our relationship ended after the first five years, the good years. All 'our' images after that, not that there would be many of us together, must be virtual. Perfect digital records, never to fade or deteriorate from all that human handling. Alive only in clouds. Like my mental plans, perfect and unable to be grasped and sullied.

This morning, I got an email from Gail. She says that she is coming over next month. She says she is beginning to think that I'll never come to Perth, never see a Parents & Friends meeting in action. She thinks I'm possibly a 'gunna'. Then immediately she apologises. 'Sorry, I know you're busy. And still getting used to living alone and fixing up the house,' she writes.

I've been quite honest with Gail. She knows about the arrangement I had with Margaret. She knows I have absolutely no contact with any of my family, except for one cousin who lives nearby in Gosford. Gail has heard of Gosford. And like a lot of people, she knows The Entrance. She holidayed there as a child. She remembers the merry-go-round by the channel, and the pelicans.

Gail once asked me about a coffee shop in Long Jetty. 'Have you been to the Obsidian Tambourine?'

It turns out that Gail has a cousin whose son works there as a barista. Seamus is his name. 'He's tall and has red hair,' she says.

I tell her I've been there a couple of times, but I don't hang out at coffee shops much. One thing I haven't told Gail is that my modus operandi, since about 2006, is to make plans and never follow through with them. She's finding that out for herself.

Gail will be visiting an old schoolfriend who lives in Asquith. She says she'd like to catch a train up to the Central Coast and meet me. 'Could you pick me up at Tuggerah?' she writes. 'I'd love to see your lagoon and what you've done with the house.'

I envisage taking Gail on a tour around the house and describing the plans for a twenty square metre mixed hardwood deck extending out the back. Then I'll tell her about the colour scheme I have planned: 'cashew nut' on the fibro, 'heritage red' for the doors and windows, and 'classic cream' on the architraves. She will hear these plans and her suspicion that I'm all talk and no action will be confirmed. I might even put 'Thinking is the Best Way to Travel' by the Moody Blues, on repeat, on the stereo. It's a lovely thought, another plan! Of course, I won't do it.

Have you ever seen those houses in the suburbs that have never been painted, or renovated, or extended, or maintained? They sit on their six or seven hundred square metre block with perhaps one shrub that has never been watered, or fertilised, or pruned. And the rest of the block is just lawn; badly maintained lawn full of paspalum, mowed only when council have notified the owners about a complaint from a neighbour. I've always admired those places. Now I have one for myself. And I've always wondered what the people are like who live in those sorts of places. I wonder about myself.

As predicted, the woman comes and sits on the bench next to me as I watch another sunset. She doesn't say anything. She just sits. We watch the sky change colour. The lagoon mirrors. The hills in the west become black and two-dimensional. Perth is only two hours behind, so the sun will be quite low there as well. The woman says nothing. I can't help but look at her. Today, I take notice. She has sharp features and wild hair. She is looking out across the water. I look away.

She doesn't ask me any questions as I thought she would. I think she has a plan – say nothing, wait for him to talk.

I look back at her again. 'What do you think should be done about the state of this lake?' I ask.

'Oh. Hello. How are you today?'

'Same as yesterday. Same as I'll be tomorrow, I guess.'

'Is that good? Or not?'

'It's good actually. And how about you?'

'I'm good. Always good.'

'Are you for or against a breakwall at The Entrance?'

'Is this a test?'

'No, just curious.'

'I think it's a test, but that's OK. A breakwall would be a spectacular failure. This is a lagoon and not a lake at all. I'm Tina, by the way.'

I watch as she speaks. She continues about the inflow of sediment and nutrients, and how it can all be accredited to human activity. The timber felling initially, then the successive agricultural pursuits in the catchment area. Dairy, then citrus and poultry. Finally, the suburban sprawl. She knows her stuff. She isn't angry and doesn't blame council. I feel an attraction to her.

Tina?

The plan to dismiss this woman with my boring tale of a Do Not Reply SMS remains a plan. A plan never to be enacted. What's going on here down by the lagoon, like all things, will take its own course.

The sun has gone now. There's a chill in the air. The always present photographers are packing up their cameras. They'll be back tomorrow. And so will I.

Tina?

What Stories Should We Be Telling Each Other in These Anxious Times?

10 October 2019

I just put a jacket on. It's cold again. Winter is having a few last laughs while we ponder a future world cooked by a carbon dioxide soaked climate. The weather, always on our minds.

When I'm one hundred and ten and the young folk ask me what it was like when modern civilisation was in full swing, I'll tell them, 'They were anxious times.'

Not long ago, I was thinking that the time was ripe for some new form of literature to appear on the scene – that the novel, novella and the short story had possibly run past their use-by date. Of course, there is flash fiction. So quick and easy as we rush around in this busy world. But is flash just fashion? A flash in the pan?

One other new trend, a genre named 'cli-fi', is speculative fiction set within the postmodern civilised world of the near future that has been ravaged by climate change. Not having read any of this new genre, I assume that some works of cli-fi paint the future as a pure dystopian hell, while others inject doses of hope into the hot and humid chaos to console our anxious souls. Maybe some of the better examples of cli-fi simply explore the perennial universal aspects of the human condition in this new paradigm where hunting and gathering and small-scale horticultural activities have by necessity returned to the daily routine.

However, will there be a new movement, and not just some new trendy commercial genre, but a whole new literary form and style that will inform and enlighten the masses as to the reasons why everything in this world is so confusing and frustrating and unfathomable? Will literary fiction be able to evolve in a new direction that will supplant our current obsessive bingeing on an endless stream of multiple seasons of multiple episodes of escapism currently available at the touch of several buttons on the remote control in our living rooms?

Will it be that this new age of literature only comes into existence when the high-tech dependent mediums go out with the lights? Who knows?

The reality we are facing is one where the world becomes an absolutely horrible place to live in, with millions, if not billions, of people suffering and dying. Will any of us, when the shit really starts hitting the fan, have the luxury of indulging in the pastime of reading? And what about writing? Will the only relevant literature produced in these times of collapse be works extracted from the ruins, such as the diaries of those who managed to find a pen and paper, and some space and time and peace, to be able to record first-hand accounts of human suffering on a scale which has never been seen before?

Or will the collapse of civilisation be slow and whimpering and, therefore, a substantially long enough era that will sustain a thriving culture of writing and reading? A literature that will portray humanity in the throes of decline, be they times of joy or mayhem, or both. At some point, human civilisation, if our species does survive, will be kicking off once again. And will the new literature be a blueprint of salvation for the next civilisation? Will humanity ever learn the lessons required to ensure that a sustainable existence cannot not ignore the limits to growth on a finite planet?

In the meantime, what stories should we be telling each other? Surely, the classic hero's journey, or the *Bildungsroman*, or the stock standard three-act drama of rising conflict to climax and denouement, are ultimately irrelevant when the largest human civilisation ever to exist on Earth is collapsing. What is the point of self-discovery, or battling evil forces, or correcting systemic injustice, when the reality is that the world as we know it is falling apart around our ears and in front of our eyes?

What stories should we be telling each other in these anxious times?

Comings and Goings

I'm sitting on the jetty with Eshan. We're drinking long necks of home brew. My home brew. It's an Irish stout. Those who know about the fall of the Das family would give me merry hell for drinking with Eshan. But I don't care. Eshan assures me that the day he was introduced to the delights of cold beer was the day his world changed for the better.

It was fifteen years ago when we beat Lisarow in the under-sixteen cricket grand final. Eshan scored a hat trick with three perfectly pitched reverse swingers. It was me who convinced him to have a beer that day, the day everything changed.

'Come on, Esh,' I said. 'One can won't hurt.'

'It's not the beer I'm worried about. It's my mum. If she ever found out.'

Browny's mum had an esky full of tinnies in the boot of her V8 Holden Commodore. She'd been supplying Browny and his mates with booze since they were fourteen. Though this practice was generally frowned upon by the other parents, the day we won the grand final, our coach, Ted, and the parents who'd watched the match, turned a blind eye to the team having just one cold beer to celebrate the victory we had worked so hard for.

I'll never forget the look on Eshan's face when he had his first taste. He told me later how he'd always imagined beer to be sweet. The way men would let out a big 'Ah!' after taking a swig in his parents' restaurant where he worked as a waiter, plus its honey colour, surely meant it had to be sweet?

Eshan got the hang of the bitter taste by the end of that first can. 'Strangely refreshing,' he said.

Despite stopping in at my place on the way home from the cricket grand final to brush our teeth to eliminate any evidence of beer breath, Mrs Das smelt it immediately. And she had this large slotted metal spoon that she'd been using to stir the sauces for that night's trade. She told me to leave. And as I stepped out of the restaurant onto the main drag, I heard the screaming start up and I cringed for Eshan. When I got home, no one asked me how things went at cricket, or smelt my breath for evidence of hooliganism. I was invisible.

Nobody saw Eshan again for a month. He didn't turn up at school and we had just started in Year 11, which supposedly was so important. Kylie Green reckoned Eshan must've been sent back to India. She was wrong of course. We found out later when he did return that he'd been sent to Sydney to spend some time with an uncle. To be set straight.

Eshan came back a different person. Until the day of the grand final, Eshan obeyed his mother without question. After the visit to his uncle, Eshan went wild. Browny became Eshan's best mate and they went out drinking and partying at every opportunity. Mrs Das ended up kicking her only son out of home. Esh's dad, Jagdish, better known as Jack, tried to talk sense into his wife, but she would have nothing to do with a no-good beer-drinking son. Browny's mum took Eshan in.

Esh and I saw less and less of each other over our senior years at school. Personally, I couldn't stand Browny. He was a bully and a spoilt brat. He got given his mum's Commodore when he turned seventeen. On Mondays, Browny and his mates would brag on about how many pingers they'd popped, and how they hadn't slept for the whole weekend. Then they'd start on about the girls who they had fingered or rooted. Most of it was bullshit, and all of it was repulsive. I made a conscious decision to distance myself as far as I could from Browny and his entourage, which now included Eshan.

Eshan would invite me to join in, but I had a girlfriend at the time and I used her as my excuse for staying indoors and well away from the gang and their usual haunt, the Beery down at Terrigal. I assumed that Eshan himself was having a ball. So much freedom, so much attention.

He was always something of a novelty in this white-Anglo outpost that is the Central Coast. He was exotic, as well as tall and good-looking.

After school, I left the area to study at Armidale in the country. Every now and then, I'd drive back home on weekends to catch up with family and friends. I would hear the local gossip. It was how I learnt that Mrs Das had closed the restaurant and returned to India; that Aisha, Esh's younger sister and only sibling, had become a Seventh Day Adventist and moved to Cooranbong; and apparently, Jack Das, who now, with no job, no wife and no kids at home, took up drinking. Years of matrimonially enforced sobriety had fermented a thirst inside Jack that would take decades and his life savings to quench.

Nobody knew much about what happened to Eshan. There was some talk that he lived in the eastern suburbs in Sydney. Kylie Green, who was still around and doing a traineeship at a beauty clinic down at The Entrance, claimed she saw Eshan one day, swimming at Gordon's Bay. She reckoned by the amount of gold bling he was wearing that he was probably dealing cocaine. But she'd been wrong before.

Five years ago, I returned to the Central Coast. I bought a two-bedroom house about halfway between the lake and the beach. You can walk to either. I was lucky and got into the housing market just before the area had a boom. Long Jetty was becoming the new hipster hotspot. I have mixed feelings about this area. There's no doubt it's geographically beautiful, and generally, the people are down to earth. But it's changing rapidly. It seems the people in power have hoodwinked us all into believing that growth is good. I fear for the lakes. The word eutrophication comes back to me from high school. While we squabble amongst ourselves over the pros and cons of a breakwall at The Entrance, parcels of vacant land are being cleared and subdivided, and classic old houses are being bulldozed for some form or other of multiple occupancy. Too many people. Too much aspiration.

So I go to work and keep my anti-growth sentiments to myself. I go fishing. I brew beer. And I keep the notion of finding a partner simmering in my imagination.

Six months ago, on an afternoon walk along the lake foreshore, I spotted Eshan Das.

There was a cold southerly blowing and he was wearing a loose white cotton shirt. Of course it was Eshan. And he was carrying a six-pack of Tooheys New – deer beer, as he used to call it. I saw in this figure the old Eshan. The Eshan who could do magic with a cricket ball to beat the best team in the comp. The Eshan who would smile as though he had not a worry in the world. The sole Indian boy in a sea of whiteness. Impervious to criticism. Impervious to the cold, and the heat.

'Eshan,' I called as he came closer.

'Hello, my old friend,' he replied and we walked together along the path that meanders through the casuarinas.

He pointed ahead and told me he was renting a place. 'Right on the lake!' He handed me a beer.

'I heard you lived in Sydney, the eastern suburbs?'

We walked and talked and came to his house. 'Come inside. I have some nuts.'

Eshan's place was an old classic. It had stone foundations and the walls were weatherboards up to hip height, and then fibro up from there. There were leadlight features in the windows and front door. The roof was tin and I noticed a chimney which was leaning slightly. Inside, I discovered that the chimney was for an old wood-burning stove.

Later, after we had eaten the nuts and finished our second beer, Eshan fired up the stove and mixed up some flour and water. 'We should eat some bread.'

The flatbread he cooked directly on the cast-iron stove top, which he drizzled with a small amount of fragrant mustard seed oil, filled the house with a homely aroma and filled our stomachs with simple goodness.

'One must eat when one drinks,' he said with a smile.

We opened our third beers. It's amazing how much information can be communicated in such a short time between two humans willing to listen and learn. Over the years, the gossip mill had ground the name Eshan Das into worthless brown dust. He had become just one more person from our collective past to join the long list of those destroyed by drugs and alcohol. Browny was on that list, and so were a few others from that gang. I was feeling somewhat uncomfortable about joining in on a drinking session with my old friend, who I now realised I had greatly missed. His easy manner, that killer smile and a genuine humility – so rare these days.

Eshan admitted to trying almost every drug available for human, or horse, consumption. But it was alcohol that did the most damage. He drank daily and to excess. He ended up addicted and unable to function without a decent belly full of lager – his own words. At the behest of a girl named Julie, he attended AA for six months. He was dry for this whole period. But he felt like shit. The meetings made him feel weak, that he had some disease. Step two, the one about submitting to a power greater than himself, only served to remind him of his mother and his uncle. He felt angry when he thought of them. AA's insistence on total abstinence did not sit well with my old friend Eshan.

I asked Esh what happened that time he was sent away to his uncle's. He recounted a story I still find hard to believe, though I know it to be true. Eshan was forced to live on alcohol alone for a whole week. He was only sixteen at the time; it would never be allowed today. Locked in a room and only given wine and spirits, he became sick. The point? Alcohol was poison. In the second week of his confinement, Eshan, still locked in a room, was force fed a so-called cleansing and revitalising Ayurvedic diet. The herbs would cause him to vomit. The uncle said purging was good and necessary, and Eshan should be grateful he had family who loved and cared for him. In the third and final week, Eshan was supplied only rice and water and told to meditate.

'To be honest,' he said, 'the week of wine and whiskey was the least disturbing for me. The one thing I did learn was that my mother and her crazy brother were fanatics. My hatred for them drove me to indulge in everything and anything that they deemed wrong or evil. You wouldn't believe what my mother would say about some of the people who came to our restaurant. She was so judgemental, so full of disgust for other humans.'

Eshan got over his rebellion. He got over Julie, and AA. He began to like himself again and after a few years of abstinence, he started drinking again. Not every day, and not to excess. He avoided spirits, and he would make sure he ate when he drank. 'Beer and unleavened bread, can't go wrong,' he laughed.

Today it is warm, summer once again. Eshan and I have become great friends, like we were years ago. I've introduced him to the dark art of luderick fishing; he is teaching me to swing bowl. Eshan is starting to catch fish; I don't think I'll ever be able to get a cricket ball to move off its normal trajectory. But I don't mind. Hanging out in the nets is great for the body and mind. And it gets a beer thirst going. Sitting on the jetty, we are planning how to save Eshan's sister, the one married to the Seventh Day Adventist. Things aren't going well for her at all, Eshan tells me.

A mullet jumps. A shag is perched on the handrail of the jetty and is drying its wings. It shits white onto the decking.

'Have you added extra hops into this stout?' asks Eshan.

'Maybe.' I used to keep meticulous records of my brewing. Now I just pump them out to keep up a regular supply.

'It tastes like it.'

Eshan has joined in with my operation and we discuss the art of brewing and the new wide range of craft beers available for consumption wherever you look. We agree that the hop fad has gone a bit too far. The XPA on tap at the Savoy, as an example, is nice for the first schooner, but one is enough.

Tomorrow, we are going to visit Eshan's father, Jack. He is down and out in Woy Woy. He has stopped drinking as he has no money left. Some church group is feeding him and providing shelter.

'You know, Eshan, I reckon your dad is going through what you went through after your mum kicked you out. You're just maybe ten years ahead of him.'

'You know, I have thought exactly that myself.' Eshan finishes his long-neck. 'Now, what are we going to call our next brew? It has to be named after some animal.'

We toss around several ideas. The next brew is a pilsener. Platypus Pilsener is sitting at the top of our list so far. We muck around a lot. We do talk about serious stuff as well. Politics and the environment being common subject areas. But we always end up laughing.

'I don't think we'll introduce Dad to our home brew just yet,' says Esh.

'Maybe not yet, but one day. Can he spin a cricket ball?'

'To be honest, I haven't a clue.'

Journalising
25 October 2019

It happens every once and a while. He writes away in his electronic journal, named El-Jo, and a story creeps in and takes over. It then gets cut and pasted into its own file, is given a title, and edited. Later maybe, it gets posted on his blog or submitted to a literary mag, or entered into a competition.

It's a good habit, this writing in a journal first thing in the morning, if there isn't some other story currently under construction. Don't look at the internet before doing this; the internet can induce mighty buzzes of anger – which only brings on venting and raving and wasting buckets of time. And what good is that?

There is a bird outside. He's heard it before. A summer bird. That's it, fig bird. He pictures its olive plumage and red beak.

His wireless keyboard is dusty and dirty, but how do you clean these things? No, don't Google that. Not now anyway.

That's right, there are some bills needing to be paid today. He sets an alarm on his phone to remind him to do it later. Later, after the morning writing session.

He hears a garbage truck and remembers he hasn't put the bins out yet. Should it be done now in case it comes down the street earlier than usual?

He goes outside and unknowingly steps with his left foot onto one end of a fallen twig from the paper bark tree above. Like an unbalanced seesaw, the other end of the twig flicks up into the air and stabs his right foot as he steps forward. His foot is bleeding, not badly. At least the smelly red garbage bin is out. He goes back to his computer and El-Jo.

He journals in third person, an attempt to get out of his own head and into the never-never world of story which is full of fictional characters waiting to be plucked out of the aether and laid down faithfully and magically onto the page. He likes this world. He gets into the zone when he enters into its mysterious timeless dimension.

Fingers go on automatic pilot. Sentences form, clumsy at first. Random adjectives attach to nouns, some are kept, others deleted. The fig bird and the garbage truck fade out. The bills and their due dates are nowhere to be found in his writing mind. The slight throb in his right foot is washed away by a splash of dopamine. He could be anywhere, in any era, of any gender, race, or sexual preference. Anything could happen.

Nothing else matters, for the moment, on this morning.

Whatever Happened to Pistols in the Piano?

I. What a Good Year for the Nectarines

Women live longer than men. Perhaps that is why we build granny flats down the back and not grandpa flats.

But some blokes buck the trend and outlive their wives. Grandpa Neville has done it, done it by a long shot. His wife, Beverly, died thirty years ago. Our kids didn't ever get to know Bev. Just as well, really; she was a sour old thing. Sixty-one when she dropped off the perch, as they say. The doctor who ended up signing the death certificate put down natural causes. They couldn't find anything wrong with her, other than being dead.

Neville is my wife's father. We built him a flat out the back and he's been there for three years now. Initially, he was a bit wary about leaving Wyong, where he'd lived for just about his whole adult life. Now, we call him the Mayor of Long Jetty. He knows everyone and everyone knows him.

'Morning, Neville,' they say as he walks Declan our dog every morning on his way to the Obsidian Tambourine, a local café. He drops off seasonal herbs in exchange for a cappuccino and a bag of yesterday's coffee grounds.

The coffee grounds are doing wonders for our sandy soil. In three years, Neville has transformed our suburban block from a weedy lawn into a productive garden. And not only that, the bloke is an absolute joy to have around. Well, at least it's a joy for me.

Everyone has their own theory on how to live a long life. I love it when you see someone on the telly who has just hit one hundred and they get asked for their secret to longevity, and they reply, 'Lots of sex,' or, 'A whisky and a cigarette every night before bed.' In the case of Neville, who most of us reckon will have no problems hitting the century, it has to be his positive attitude that keeps him ticking.

'No one likes a whinger,' answers Neville whenever he is ever asked about his unshakeable sunny disposition.

Lately, I've had a lot more time on my hands so I've been visiting Neville in his grandpa flat. I walk out my front door and onto the nature strip. I turn left and then left again to go down the driveway to his place.

My wife asks why I don't just go out the back and cross the vegie garden that spans the agreed upon boundary between our patch and his.

I say, 'It's important to have boundaries. Have you noticed your dad does the same? He never just walks up to our back door.'

'You men,' she says and shakes her head.

My wife, Sarah, shakes her head a lot. She is still working full-time, whereas I have scaled down my hours. It's called transitioning to retirement and I draw upon some of my superannuation. Sarah thinks I'm mad, that I'm jeopardising my future. But I was dying at work.

Neville and I talk about all sorts of things as we sit out on the little veranda that runs along the front of his flat. We drink tea and dunk biscuits. I'm getting to really know my father-in-law, finally. I'm finding out how similar we are. It makes me wonder if Sarah married her father, so to speak.

One day, Neville said to me, 'You know, Sarah is just like her mother.'

I didn't know what to say in response. A cold feeling ran down the inside of my left arm.

'Some people, for some reason I have no idea about, are full of fear. And be blowed if I know how you fix that.'

'Sarah does worry a lot, that's for sure,' I said.

'Yep, worry. Serves no useful purpose at all, if you ask me. It eats your insides out.'

'I've been trying to get Sarah to go part-time at work. But then again I'm not sure what she'd do with all the extra time on her hands.'

'There's nothing you can do. I see how you are with her. It reminds me of myself with Beverly. No matter what I did, she always saw the negative side of things. To be honest, if she hadn't died so young, I think I would've eventually left her. Once Sarah and her brother left home, and she had less people to worry about, she really homed in on me. I kept thinking, when is she going to change, when is she going to wake up and see that everything's fine and not going to fall apart, or crash and burn? When is she going to be happy and enjoy life?'

I've often thought about leaving my wife. When our youngest left home, I thought now would be good – I couldn't use staying together for the sake of the kids as an excuse any more. But now, I look at our money situation and use that as my excuse for hanging in. All our wealth is tied up in this family home, especially now since we built the grandpa flat out the back.

If unhappiness and discontent are bad for your health, there's a good chance Sarah could die at sixty-one, just like her mother. It's only a year away. But that's wishful thinking, and I can't help feeling guilty when I think it. But it doesn't stop me thinking it. Anyway, she could and probably will live on forever. I can see myself in the future, lying in hospital, dying of some preventable disease that I didn't bother getting screened for. And there's Sarah, standing the way she does, scolding me for being slack about my health. She's worrying about being left alone, she'll tell me how she never ever thought she'd become a widow. And then she'll tell me how she's worrying about having no one to worry about any more!

There's a few old fruit trees on our block at Long Jetty. Before we built the flat out the back, before Neville moved in, he would visit us occasionally, like for the kids' birthdays and for Christmas and whatnot, and he'd look at these tired old trees and ask if we ever got any fruit. I told him how the citrus always got leaf miner and stink bugs and how the stone fruit was always ruined by fruit fly. I remember at the time Neville agreeing how these pests were tricky things to deal with.

I also remember the day after Neville moved into the flat, he came to our front door and asked if he could spray the citrus trees on our section of the now divided block. 'I've done the mandarin on my side,' he said.

'Go for it,' I said.

He sprayed the orange tree and the lemon tree; he picked off the infected leaves and binned them. A few days later, he was asking if he could work on the other trees; he pruned the plum, peach and nectarine trees. He fertilised and mulched. He listened to music on a Bluetooth wireless speaker as he worked. I had to ask him how that worked, as I was a complete technophobe.

He pulled his mobile phone out of his pocket and showed me the Spotify app. 'How good is this new technology?' he said.

You'd think I might be embarrassed about getting a lesson on apps and Bluetooth from an eighty-seven-year-old, but I was never embarrassed around Neville. Though I often felt inadequate and ignorant after a session with him. But that's my stuff.

In 1970, Neville moved with his young family to Wyong from Sydney. Sarah was eleven at the time and she has never forgiven her father for leaving the city and moving to what she calls Hicksville. She blames the move for her brother's demise and also for the chronic melancholy suffered by her mother. 'Can you imagine what it would've been like for a woman born and bred in Vaucluse to have to suddenly make a new life in Wyong? In 19-bloody-70?' Neville admitted it was big change for everyone. And he told me how Beverly was the one who initially wanted to move away from Sydney or, more specifically, to move away from her pretentious and controlling mother. Neville made the best of it; his wife remained a victim. Now I'm married to Sarah, the next generation. How did Neville and I both not see what we were marrying? For peace of mind, in my case, I put it down to being young and stupid and thinking that a person needs a life partner. Besides, everyone else my age was getting married, and that is what you do, isn't it? It's a poor excuse, but it's the truth.

With the fruit tree recovery and Neville's other gardening expertise, it wasn't long before we were regularly eating homegrown produce. I love cooking and had always done the lion's share of it at home. Now I had fresh seasonal vegetables and access to every herb you could ever want for.

There was a loose arrangement that Neville would come over every Thursday night for dinner. Sometimes, one or both of our kids would come over, perhaps with or without whatever partner they had at the time, and we'd have a big family meal.

More often than not, as I farewell my daughter out the front as she gets into her car, she asks, 'What's wrong with Mum?'

I can't answer her as I don't know. But it makes me feel better that I'm not the only one noticing her melancholy.

Neville and I are sitting at the firepit. It's a Friday night and we are burning the last bits of the fallen-down fence, drinking beer, eating nuts and reflecting on the week that was. I do most of my part-time hours on Fridays, a choice I made to preserve that precious end of the working week feeling.

Sarah came out earlier to ask if I had any thoughts about dinner.

I told her that there was plenty of stew left from last night's family get together and she could go ahead and heat some up for herself. 'Don't wait for me,' I said.

She shook her head and said we were mad, sitting outside in the cold.

'Hey, Neville, tell me again about the time when you set up that computer for the council back in the seventies.'

'Really? You want to hear that again?'

'Yeah, I'm trying to write it all down. I think it's a history that shouldn't be lost and forgotten. Plus, it's a great yarn.'

I throw another section of hardwood fence post onto the fire and orange sparks spiral up into the crisp night air. Neville and I cut up the last of the posts on Tuesday morning. He reckoned, 'He who cuts firewood gets warm twice.' I was buggered by the time we finished and couldn't believe how my father-in-law trotted off to line dancing at the Senior Citizens Club. And how he came home later with Silvia, the young Argentinian septuagenarian. Then at eight p.m., I heard Neville's car start up and reverse out of the carport. I assumed he was taking Silvia home to Nareen Gardens Retirement Village. I wonder if Neville needs Viagra. I know he has praised the wonders of modern medical science more than once. Neville, always positive.

'Great idea to write this stuff down. You know you're right, the council would have no records from this era,' says Neville.

A few years after Neville and his family moved from the eastern suburbs in Sydney to Wyong on the Central Coast, he landed a job with the council as a plumber. The security of full-time employment enabled Neville and Beverly to get a loan from the bank to buy a home on a large block on the east side of the railway tracks. Beverly always complained about the house they bought. 'Too cold. Too close to the river. Too small.' She would go on and on about it. Until she stopped going on, that was.

'It was '76 when council made everyone do that aptitude test,' says Neville.

Great, I think. I couldn't remember that year date. Must remember it now.

'Hang on, Neville.' I interrupt. 'Can you just wait a bit while I duck inside and get a pen and paper. I want to get some of these details down.'

'Sure, you can duck into my place if you want. There's a pen and pad on the dining table.'

'Thanks, mate. I'll go to mine. I'll check in on Sarah.'

'You're a good man, Smiddy.'

Inside, Sarah has the gas heater on and is watching TV. 'So you're finished out there?' she asks. 'Can you do the stew? I'm so tired after work.'

'I was actually just getting a pen and paper and going back out. But I can heat up a bowl for you.'

'Don't bother,' she says. 'What do you too old fools talk about all the time anyway?'

'Well, I might be an old fool, but your father's not. I don't know why you can't see that.'

'Don't tell me about my own father. Go on then, go and talk rubbish. And if I'm in bed when you get back, don't disturb me. It might be best if you sleep in the spare room. Please.'

Gladly, I think. The way she says please irks me no end. 'OK, darling,' I reply and skirt away before she can dump on me further.

I head back outside with paper and pen and sit down across from Neville. 'OK, ready now,' I say.

He is staring straight ahead. I can see the fire reflected in his glasses. He is thinking about dates and other details, I'm thinking. I wait for a bit, expecting him to start the story again.

What I do remember is that Neville, like everybody who worked for the council, from the general manager to the tea ladies, were all given the same test. Six people, including Neville and one of the tea ladies, Margaret, who now lives Port Douglas and who Neville still maintains contact with, scored high enough on the test and were selected to become computer programmers. They were sent off to Hornsby TAFE to do six months training. The aim was for this crew to come back to council and to program the new truck-sized computer that had been installed by IBM in a room on the second floor of the council building. Its only function was to print out the rate notices for the next year. And every ratepayer had to have their details punched into a card that would then be fed by hand into the mouth of this monster.

'Neville,' I say, 'are you awake?'

Neville is asleep, or lost in thought.

'Neville?'

No response. He's asleep.

I stand up and go over to him. I'll help him into bed. I grip him on the shoulder. He slides away from me and falls to the ground, dead!

After the funeral, Sarah says to me, 'Pity no one has the guts to tell the truth about the dead.'

'What do you mean?' I ask.

I sort of know what she means; people do tend to gild the funeral lilies. Often, out of respect for the dead, a lot of stuff does remain unsaid. Well known, but unsaid. I get that, but I want to know exactly what she means. Because today, as far as I'm concerned, every speaker gave an honest account of Neville. There was nothing bad to say. He was the genuine article.

'Well, how about Dad moving the whole family up to Wyong for a start?'

'Wasn't that because Beverly wanted to get away from her mother?'

'That's rubbish,' she says. 'Mum never got over being dumped in that forever cold house while Dad was away at work living the life of Reilly.'

'You're kidding, aren't you? Your mother never made an effort. She was damaged long before Wyong.'

'You don't know what you're talking about.'

At the wake, I had a lovely conversation with Michael, Sarah's brother. Sarah blames her father for the troubles that Michael has had with alcohol and drugs over the years. What Sarah seems to conveniently forget is that Neville stayed on working at the council until he was seventy-five so that he could pay for all the rehab that Michael went through. She also seems to forget that Michael has been sober and off the drugs for fifteen years, and has steady employment, and a wife and baby he adores. And if she spoke to her brother, which she refuses to do, she would, if she could open her ears, hear a very different account of their father and their childhood.

'All right, Sarah,' I say, 'apart from the move to Wyong, OK, tell me one other thing about your father that should have been said at the funeral today?'

Silence. She is trying to think of something.

'OK. I'll make it easier for you.' I'm getting angry now. I can't quite believe that Neville is gone. I thought he'd make a hundred at least. 'Tell me one thing that anyone said about your father today that was bullshit. Just one.'

Silence.

I go to leave.

She says, 'There's no point. You don't understand.'

She's right. I don't understand, and I'm grieving, and I decide right now to to give up trying to understand this woman. And I will give up waiting for her to change, or die. I'm going to move out to the granny flat. And I'm going to set up my drums. Martin, an old mate, is talking about getting the band back together.

This year, my daughter has Christmas lunch at her place in Terrigal. She loves cooking and she has a brand-new boyfriend. He seems like a nice bloke. My son comes over by himself. He has just split up with his girlfriend of eighteen months, the longest one so far. I'm happy that both my kids are not settling down with someone just because that is what you do. They are at that age. They talk about engagements and weddings they have attended. I know some of the friends they talk about. I entertain the thought that Sarah and I have taught our kids what a marriage should not be like.

Over lunch, Sarah talks on and on about the dangers of 5G. I can see my kids looking at each other and rolling their eyes. My son tries to top up his mother's wine glass.

She stops him. 'I have to drive, don't I?' she says as she looks at me.

We came separately.

My moving out the back into Neville's place, apparently, is the cause of Sarah's depression. Supposedly, Sarah's been seeing a counsellor. My daughter told me this.

My daughter is angry with her mother. 'I bet she hasn't even seen anyone, Dad.'

After lunch, Sarah feigns a migraine and leaves. No one is surprised or overly concerned. And I sense the relief all round. Neville and I used to talk about nature versus nurture a lot. He believed that his wife Beverly must have suffered some great trauma as a child, so great that she was never able to heal. He also believed that somehow Beverly's melancholy was passed onto Sarah. It could've been genetic in this case, or perhaps it was from the nurturing. Who's to know, he would say.

I go to the kitchen and get the fruit platter that I brought along as my contribution to the lunch. There are figs, peaches, plums and nectarines, all from the home garden. I have vowed to myself to keep these trees and the vegie and herb gardens going, in honour of Neville. I've also been line dancing on Tuesdays. Silvia is teaching me some Spanish.

Always a good eater, my son tucks into the fruit. 'Well,' he says, 'some would say that it's been a shit of a year. I've lost another girlfriend. Grandpa Nev kicked the bucket. Mum and Dad have split up, finally. But you could say that none of this really matters in the big picture, because it's been a bloody good year for the nectarines. Well done, Dad.'

II. Meet Me at the Charcoal Chicken Shop

There's a little army in black polo shirts that runs the charcoal chicken shop on the main road near my home. I don't know if I like what I see or not – all that regimental routine and obvious hierarchy. But there's no denying the chickens are top class. I'm buying one for a picnic dinner down by the lake.

There used to be two charcoal chicken shops in Long Jetty. They were across the road from each other. Local gossip has it that initially there was one shop and the operators, the black shirts, had some troubles with the landlord, so they relocated across to the other side of the main road. The abandoned landlord then decided to run his own charcoal chicken shop. So, for a brief period, there was this situation with two identical businesses within plain sight of each other. Eventually, the original operators in their new premises won the unofficial Long Jetty Charcoal Chicken Competition. The newly installed people in the old shop, despite discounting the shit out of their chickens, went bust and disappeared.

Talk about having two of the same business in the one suburb: Long Jetty has two chemists, two drive-through bottleshops, two vets, two Seven-Elevens, two dental practices, two dance schools, two aquarium shops, two Indian restaurants and two tattoo parlours. Bucking the trend of twos, there are three Chinese restaurants and seven coffee shops. Apparently, there is no limit as to how many coffee shops a suburb can sustain. And to complete the picture, there are some businesses that are one-offs, like the Christmas shop that operates all year round, the teeny weeny post office, the brothel, and the hair lice eradication centre.

Presently, there is no bakery, no menswear, no shoe shop, no greengrocer and no bookshop. You can buy loaves of bread from the Obsidian Tambourine, one of the seven cafés. My wife, Tina, brought one home the other day; it cost eight bucks. It tasted good, but eight bucks! I'm waiting for a proper bakery with cheaper bread and a selection of cakes that would include Neenish tarts and Chelsea buns. And you can buy shoes, dead person shoes probably, from the second-hand clothing shop. The General Store, which has a great range of Asian spices, does have a small selection of fruit and veg that can be found in the refrigerated cabinet halfway along the right hand wall, if you're looking.

Once, Long Jetty had a methadone clinic, just one. Heaps of Central Coast people know this. Some people still call the suburb Long Junkie. Tina told her sister in Tasmania about it. Her sister didn't have a clue about where this so-called Central Coast was. Over the phone, Tina explained to her that it's in between Sydney and Newcastle. I've heard people call it Mt Druitt by the Sea, or B-grade Sydney. I like being in B-grade, less wankers.

I have a friend, Henry, who is moving to Long Jetty, along with Svetlana, his Russian doll.

It's definitely not politically correct to call a woman a doll, but let me explain. Henry met Svetlana online. The website was called Russian Doll. And more than that, when Henry has come up to the Central Coast the last few times, to see the area, to check out houses for sale and whatnot, he has been bringing Svetlana along. Each time she comes, I see another side to her. It's just like opening up a Russian doll. The first time it was all red hair and this Babushka accent. The next time, she pointed at a crimson rosella in a casuarina and squealed with excitement. Then one time they came up and stayed at the Ibis Hotel, which is attached to the RSL club called Diggers. That night, she hoed into a rare rump steak and sang 'Love Will Tear Us Apart' at karaoke. The next day, she picked up a handful of soil in my backyard and said it would be good for growing potatoes. Tina calls Svetlana a live wire — there's certainly many layers.

Anyway, Henry has exchanged contracts on this blue fibro box in Pacific Street. It's walking distance from our place. I imagine once he and his new bride move in, we'll get to see more and more Russian dolls inside Svetlana. I even imagine that one day we might well indeed find a teeny weeny KGB operative at the very core. Lo and behold, could this Russian email-order bride service be nothing other than Putin's latest attempt at foreign interference to weaken Western democracies? I trust Henry knows what he's doing.

I order one charcoal chicken. There's plenty of them cooked and ready to go in the heated display cabinet. You'd think that the person who took my order and processed my Paywave transaction could simply pick up the tongs and slide a chook into one of those foil-lined bags and hand it to me. I mean, there's no one behind me waiting to order. But it doesn't work that way, not in this shop. The order is pinned up and someone else will take care of my chicken. I'm always bemused by all the other customers in the shop sitting down and waiting for their orders, because I know from experience that I'll get my chicken soon from one of the more senior persons in a black polo shirt. The people sitting down must be waiting for chips, or other deep-fried food to be cooked, and not just wanting a barbecue chook. I never buy the other food available from this shop, just the chicken.

My Tina has agoraphobia, though she can go out at twilight and night-time. Her agoraphobia is a daylight phenomenon. Tina presses flowers and makes cards and books and other items of stationery that she sells online through Etsy. She's a whizz on the computer. She does my tax online. I'm a lucky man.

I'm taking the chicken and a garden salad that Tina has made down to the lakeside. Henry and Svetlana are coming. Tina said she might wander down later if she feels up to it. Henry and Svetlana are bringing bread and beer and the picnic set that lives in the boot of his car. I drop into the bottle shop and get a bottle of red just in case Tina makes it down later. She'd like that, a drop of red.

When I go out by myself because of Tina's condition, she always makes me feel fine about leaving her home alone. She is such a giving and forgiving person. She takes responsibility for everything and everyone. To some extent, that is the core of her problem, and she knows it, but she accepts it as part of the deal. She says she has never been so happy since she has met me. 'Go, go,' she says. 'Enjoy yourself. I'll be fine, don't worry about me.'

I've been doing some research on the local history of the Central Coast, and Long Jetty in particular. I drove out to Tuggerah to access the local history resources held by the public library. The Tuggerah branch is located in a whopping big Westfield shopping centre. Soon, everything will be located in shopping centres. I reckon it won't be long before the churches and the courthouses set up shop like everyone else. You will be able to be christened, married, divorced, convicted and sentenced, all within easy reach of Aldi and Big W. How convenient. The one or two people who are making squillions of dollars out of shopping centres, who some-bloody-how get even richer when retail sales are falling, must hate places like Long Jetty and the other little suburban villages that are having a revival. All that hipster commerce, something will have to be done about that, they scheme.

Local history sections in libraries typically have filing cabinets with vertical files, microfiche readers and shelves of books and other material that is NOT FOR LOAN. It's too precious to be lost. You have to do your study in situ. I guess one good thing about the library being in the shopping centre is that you can duck out and get a doughnut, or pop in to the bulk billing medical centre to check if the results of the biopsy done on that lump on your head have come back. Everything under one roof.

It makes sense these history materials are NOT FOR LOAN. Our history is full of gaps. We can't afford to lose what fragments we have managed to hang onto. So much never collected in the first place. There's bugger all about Long Jetty other than some bits and pieces that I already knew. And there's virtually nothing about the Indigenous peoples who once inhabited this coastal area. Tens of thousands of years of oral history wiped out by germs and iron, arrogance and ignorance.

I'll tell Henry what I did manage to pick up about Bungaree and the last full-blooded Aboriginal, Billy Fawkner, who died in 1875. Apparently, he drowned in Tuggerah Lake. I'll tell Henry there's records of resistance. Yes, we invaded and stole the land. There was a familiar pattern. Firstly, tall timber was felled and shipped back to the mother country, next, the bringing in of foreign plants and animals to please the European palates. No consideration for the native peoples or the native ecosystems. I'll tell Henry how the shoreline on which we will picnic was once a haven of white sands and abundant prawns. They built the jetties – Long Jetty has three of them – to assist the disembarkation of holidaymakers from Sydney who came by train and ferry. Now, the jetties slowly rot and the shoreline is racked with wrack, and smelling accordingly. I'll tell Henry how one night Tina and I spotted a fox scavenging for garbage.

The day I went to the library at the shopping centre, I forgot where I parked my car. I walked around for a good half an hour till I found it. I was off centre. My mission to educate myself about the local history for the sake of Henry, my old friend and soon to be new neighbour, had been a failure. It had once again stirred up my anger with the whole situation regarding the lack of action in regard to reconciliation with this land's first human inhabitants. The recent dismissal of the Uluru

Statement from the Heart by the current government made me so angry that if I let it consume me, I end up crying. I have absolutely no fucking idea what to do about it. The idea of moving to New Zealand has crossed my mind. And when Tina and I recently visited there for a holiday, she didn't have one moment of agoraphobia.

I've got the bottle of red. I hope Tina comes down and joins us. When her agoraphobia flares up, she starts putting sarongs and scarves over the windows and the glass panels in the front and back doors. She says that the light gives her a headache. When I'm out in the bright light, I often bring home flowers that I find on my travels. I'm pretty sure the Norfolk Island hibiscus trees are flowering at the moment, so I must remember to pick some for her.

Today, Svetlana seems withdrawn and a bit moody – another doll? I hope things are working out for her and Henry. It took a lot of rigmarole to get Svetlana out here.

No one has bought along any tongs, so how to tear the chicken up becomes bit of a problem. I say I don't mind if someone does it with their hands. Henry volunteers and goes to pick up the chook, which is steaming away on the ripped opened bag. Svetlana stops him. She gets the plastic carry bag and puts her hands into the two bottom corners and rips the chicken apart into quarters. She's done that before.

'Take one part home for Tina,' she says.

I start telling Henry and Svetlana what I know about the jetties. Watkins Jetty is the closest. It was built in the 1920s. That much is written on the plaque that stands nearby. There is a photo of a boarding house, also built by Watkins, called Elsimere. I have a photo of it on my computer at home. I tell Henry I can email it to him. I figure that this guest house stood about right where we are sitting eating charcoal chicken, salad and bread rolls. The meal and the local history must seem pretty mundane for a gal from the Russian steppe.

I apologise to Svetlana for the boring local history lesson.

She says, 'No,' and apologises herself, explaining how she is distracted. She has just found out her brother in Omsk has cancer. She takes a swig of beer.

Two women come walking along the path. They must be in their late twenties, early thirties. Just girls really. They are well dressed and are carrying glasses of white wine. It looks like they have wandered off from a function of some sort. A wedding reception? Maybe. They are drunk, they swagger. They walk past and over to the old shed that once hired out catamarans and paddle boats when the lake wasn't choked with wrack. They sit on the ramp and finish off their wines. One of them is crying.

Svetlana takes an interest in the two women while I rattle off the family names of nearby streets – Stella, Thelma, Albert. They form part of the subdivision called Watkins Estate. Henry notices the black swans out on the lake. I think about a Dreamtime story I've heard. It tells how the swan got its black feathers, white wing tips and red beak. But I'll save that story for another time; after Henry and Svetlana have moved up here.

The crying girl is becoming inconsolable. Her friend puts her arm around her but is shrugged off. She stands up and cries at the sky. Then, she walks down the wooden ramp and steps off straight into the water. It is only knee deep. Her friend calls her back, but the distraught girl, drunk on wine and overcome by whatever trauma has surfaced, walks away, out to deeper water. Svetlana stands up and grabs Henry by the shoulder.

'She's going to have to walk a long way before she gets to any deeper water,' I say. 'There's a drop off – "the step" they call it. It's way out where the jetty ends.'

The friend is calling out, 'Come back, Franca. Come back!'

Franca pushes on despite the difficulty with lifting her feet out of the sludge on the bottom. And to think this was all once white sand where people swam and frolicked and caught more prawns than you could ever eat. This section of the lake is pretty well good for nothing now. It's so clogged up with weed it would be hard even to drown yourself.

Franca's friend gives up on trying to call Franca back. She comes over to us. 'She's going to kill herself! What do we do?'

We have become a 'we' – the friend plus the set of bystanders watching a well dressed intoxicated young woman wading out into a eutrophying lake with the intention of drowning herself. There's no way I'm going to walk out into the sludge. I ask if Franca definitely said she was going to kill herself. The answer is affirmative.

Svetlana comforts the distraught friend. 'No worry. Fine it will be. Henry, get her,' she says.

Henry gives Svetlana a you're kidding look.

The commotion is attracting attention. A group of men come out of the nearby caravan park. One of then comes over to us. He also asks what can we do.

Tourists with cameras that have come to take sunset photos are pointing at Franca and at us. They don't know what to do.

I walk down to the water's edge and call out. 'Franca. Come back!'

She turns and looks at me. She has heard. She turns back and starts pulling her legs out of the sucking mud and plodding out towards the step.

'Come back or we will have to call the police.'

She doesn't even turn this time.

I call out, 'OK. I'm calling the police now.' I walk back to the picnic table and pick up my phone.

Henry tells me that Svetlana is worried about involving the police.

I assure him it is the right thing to do, that I have done training on suicide prevention. I check one more time, 'Did she actually say she was going to kill herself?'

The answer is yes, once again.

I dial 000.

Franca's friend is relieved that something is happening. We are doing something.

While waiting for the police, we learn that Franca has recently split up with her fiancé and going to a wedding has triggered her grief. We also learn that the group of men who have come out of the caravan park are a roofing team from Melbourne. Apparently, there is a shitload of insurance work still not completed since the hailstorm last April.

Two photographers come over to see if there is anything they can do. They are from Taiwan, we learn. Henry offers them a beer. I'm standing in this group and in my head I can't help but hear this silly melodramatic voice-over: *The Girl in the Water*, the latest blockbuster movie, directed by Quentin Tarrantino and adapted from the *New York Times* bestselling novel of the same name. Out of tragedy, a community come together to discover what they have in common is more important than their obvious differences.

'Look. She's heading over to the jetty.'

Franca has given up on ending it all. She's heading towards a stainless steel ladder that the council have attached to the side of the hundred-year-old timber jetty. Probably attached as a matter of public safety. Old Watkins would be smiling in his grave, I reckon.

Franca's friend, a few of the roofers and the two Taiwanese photographers make their way out along the jetty to meet up with the girl in the water. A couple of the roofers go back to their cabin and come back with some towels. The sky is turning orange. The weekend nearly over.

The police arrive just as Franca is helped up onto the jetty. The imminent danger is over. Like I did, the policewoman confirms that Franca did actually say that she intended to kill herself. The constable informs Franca that she will have to be taken to Wyong Hospital and assessed.

Franca, cold and wet, draped in towels, screams, 'What! No! I'm fine, just let me go home.'

'I'm sorry, Franca,' says the policewoman, 'we have to make sure you'll be OK. They'll just keep you for twenty-four hours and then you'll be able to go home.'

'Nooo! I can't go there. I have to start a new job tomorrow. I'm a teacher. I can't miss my first day. Please, please, I'm fine. I'm not suicidal, I'm just a bit drunk and upset.'

Franca throws off the towels and grabs her friend. 'Come on. Let's just go. They can't make me. Let's go.'

The policewoman apologises again and secures Franca's arm. The male officer, who has said nothing so far, secures the other arm and they begin to move her towards the paddy wagon. Franca backpedals with her muddied feet. Her friend tries to console her as she is led away.

Svetlana looks at me. I see a new doll. I shrug.

'Why did you call police? What vere you zinking?'

I've been trying to get as many people as I know to move to Long Jetty. I'm trying to build a community ever since I met Tina down by the lake at sunset. She has changed my life for the better. Ironically, the girl with agoraphobia has helped me to connect again with the world. Some people have said Tina's mad and it's not agoraphobia at all, that she's made it up. But isn't agoraphobia all in your head anyway? Who cares what variation you have. Tina can go out in the early morning and the late afternoon. It's just in the middle of the day that she shuts herself away from the marketplace of this crazy world. And yes, she can be outside all day when we are overseas. Even in Asia, in the busiest of places, she has no fear or anxieties. We once entertained the idea of moving to Bali, or Thailand. But Tina doesn't want me to have to change my country for her. She says she thinks she can get better and, even if she doesn't, she is as happy as she has ever been.

It doesn't look like Tina is coming down to join us at the lake. I'll take the bottle of red wine home and the portion of the meal that Svetlana has put together.

The paddy wagon leaves. Franca's friend comes over to me and thanks me. She says she thinks I did the right thing and now she has to go back to the wedding reception to tell others what has happened. I look at Svetlana but she is looking away, out across the water. The sky is changing colour again.

Henry changes the subject. 'So, we going to get the band back together, or what? Smiddy will be in.'

'We'll need a singer, can't imagine Lip coming back from Belgium.'

Svetlana turns around. 'I can zing.'

'I know, I've heard you. You're good. Do you like the Red Hot Chilli Peppers?'

Henry laughs. Svetlana starts singing 'Under the Bridge' without a trace of accent.

There's a plan: rehearsals on Wednesday nights, just for fun, see what happens.

Henry picks at the chicken bones on his plate. 'This chicken is bloody good,' he says.

'Did I tell you that Long Jetty once had two charcoal chicken shops?'

Svetlana tunes in. She wants to know more about this place. My concern that she might not be right for Henry, that she might not be right for Long Jetty, dissipates.

'Hello, you lot.' Tina has turned up.

I take out the bottle of red. Svetlana takes the cling wrap off Tina's plate. Henry grabs some more beers out of the esky.

It's a spectacular sunset today. The multicoloured sky reflects on the mirror surface of the lake. The tourists are snapping away. Franca will be nearly at the hospital by now. They will assess her. She will no doubt assess herself. I'm sure the school will take her on one day late. I wonder if it's where I once taught. All those years ago.

If you want to come and live in Long Jetty, come and see me. Meet me at the charcoal chicken shop on the main road. It's as good as place as any to get your bearings and a feel for the joint.

III. Dog, Martin?

My friend Martin has a problem. Tina, his wife, wants to travel the world. Martin, though, wants to put as much money as he can into funding an early retirement. Not only is he over work, he also has a philosophical objection to international travel. Martin has always been like this, perhaps a bit of an over-thinker, but always wanting to do the right thing. Ethical, he is.

'I can't stand it when you meet some so-called woke person and they're spouting all these environmental and ethical reasons for adopting plant-based diets, as well as calling out racism and white privilege all over the place, and you know that next month they're off to Europe for six weeks.'

Martin and I are sitting at the local having a few schooners of Resch's in memory of our old mate Blinky, who died of cancer way too early. Blinky used to be our sound guy back in the 80s when Martin and I were in a band together.

'I don't know what to say to Tina, Smiddy. And with her condition and all, how can I deny her?' Martin is in a bind.

'Righto,' I say, 'give me some time to think about it. We'll have a chat on Wednesday, at rehearsal, eh?'

We're trying to get the band back together. Well, not the exact same band, our lead singer Lip lives in Belgium and isn't coming home any-time soon. But three out of four is close. Henry, the other original member of Pistols in the Piano, has just moved up from Sydney and his new wife Svetlana sings like a demon. She is a fitting replacement for Lip, wild and raw, talented. Martin and I have shared a knowing look once or twice at band practice.

Martin met Tina five years ago. He met her down by the lake at sunset. After Martin split up with Margaret, his de facto of fifteen years, he vowed to live alone for the rest of his life. Yeah, right. For such a smart bloke, he can be pretty dumb at times. He also told me how he would never again make plans. He reckoned plans were a recipe for dis-aster. I pointed out to him how this all sounded like a plan. He laughed at himself. I like that about a person, the ability to laugh at oneself.

I was happy when Martin split with Margaret. They had this ar-rangement of sorts and lived pretty much totally separate lives. One shouldn't judge other couples and how they get on. My marriage is a farce, so who am I to judge? But Margaret always irked me. I couldn't put a finger on it, perhaps it was all the make-up, perhaps it was the way she walked – quickly and with tiny steps. I don't know, I just knew that overall Martin was way better off without Margaret and their arrangement. And Tina, well, she is just lovely.

Martin confides in me at times. 'Pillow talk,' he says, even though we don't sleep together.

As we have gotten older, we share a lot of stuff that as younger men we wouldn't dare talk about, or admit to. And that's how I know about Tina's condition. She has a kind of agoraphobia, her own special brand of it. Her psychiatrist even wrote a paper about it. Tina's fear of the marketplace is confined to full daylight hours. She can go out with no anxiety at dawn and dusk, and at night-time. You'll never see Tina out in the middle of the day. She even has to draw the curtains in the home she's made with Martin. For a living, she makes greeting cards and other stationery with pressed flowers. She collects the flowers on her twilight walks. And how about this? When overseas, Tina's agoraphobia disappears completely. It's the weirdest thing. I asked Martin once if she would be OK in Tasmania. He laughed. Apparently she is fine there as well.

Understandably, Tina wants to do more travelling overseas.

'I don't get it,' says Martin. 'Everyone says you just have to go to Europe. Why? Isn't it crowded and expensive and aren't the locals pissed off with hordes of tourists tromping all over their backyards? And haven't eleven thousand scientists just agreed that air travel is a significant cause of climate change?'

I nod. Martin makes good points.

'I know it has history and all, like centuries of the stuff, but seriously, with the world on the verge of collapse, how can one justify such extravagance while billions of humans can't afford to travel at all? It's kind of like going to the bar on the *Titanic* after it has hit the iceberg, one last tipple before we sink into the freezing ocean. Hang on, not perhaps my best example, but what about the irony of thousands of people travelling by planes all over the world to see a glacier, or a polar bear, before there's none left? Hello, world! I don't want to be a part of it, Smiddy.'

Martin is on a roll. I indicate it's my shout and I leave him drawing circles with his finger in the condensation that has pooled on the table from our beer glasses. I order two more and grab a couple of coasters. They reckon humidity will be the big killer. As I return, Martin is hunched over. I've seen this posture before, it's Martin taking on responsibility for other people's happiness and well-being. He does it all week, working in welfare down at The Entrance. He's a better man than I.

'But I can fully appreciate why Tina wants to go. Imagine having agoraphobia and knowing that all you have to do is fly overseas for relief. I'm surprised she doesn't want to move overseas permanently.'

'I think she knows Long Jetty is your home, Martin. She'd never expect you to up stumps and leave. She loves you, I say.'

Martin and I finish our beers and head home. Me to my granny flat, Martin home to Tina. I live out the back of the family home. My wife, Sarah, broods away in the main house. This is my dilemma: a sort of separation, a sort of compromise with Sarah, a sort of a mess is what it really is. No togetherness any more, and certainly no freedom. Freedom should be the best thing about breaking up. How can either of us properly move on when we both share the same address? Here I am trying to solve Martin's problem while I should be trying to figure out my next move.

The next morning, I take Declan, our dog, down to Shelly Beach. I see Martin and Tina getting into their car. I know the gig. They've already had their walk and Tina needs to get home. It's about six-thirty and her agoraphobia will kick in soon. Poor Tina.

Down on the beach, the idea comes to me. I don't know if it's the ozone, or just the general environment where the sea meets the land, but honestly, I get most of my ideas on the beach.

Martin has told me how Tina is always pestering him about getting a dog. 'Dog, Martin?' she says. It has become such a frequent request it has been condensed into two words. 'Dog, Martin?'

'It will wreck the garden,' he advises. And, 'We can't do anything till that fence gets fixed, and you know what a tight-arse our neighbour is?' And best of all, 'What about all this travelling you want to do? We can't get a dog and just take off to Europe.'

To be honest, I don't know why Martin hasn't come up with the idea himself. Get a dog, Martin. In fact, take mine. Take Declan. He won't wreck the garden, he's well past his digging days. I'll even come around and help mend the side fence. I love Declan, but we only got him for the sake of the kids, and they've left home. And Sarah wouldn't walk Declan in a pink fit, and she gets into a few of those. It would free me up as well. I've been thinking about spending some time with my brother down in Sydney, and Declan has been an anchor. Now, Declan can be your anchor, Martin.

At band rehearsal, we're practising 'Californication' by the Red Hot Chilli Peppers. Henry has always loved the Peppers. Svetlana is having some trouble remembering the lyrics. In a fluster, she heads out of the shed to get some air. Henry follows.

'Hey, Martin,' I say, 'I think you should get a dog. I think that might be the answer. Tina wants one, and who knows, it might quell her desire to travel. You can have Declan.'

Martin looks at me. I know the look. I've seen it a squillion times. It's his how-dumb-am-I? look. He laughs and puts his head in his hands. 'Der!' he says. 'Of course, get a dog!'

The morning after rehearsal, down at the beach, Tina asks again, 'Dog, Martin?'

Martin replies, 'Sure.'

I get the call and drop Declan around later in the afternoon. Martin and Tina take Declan for a twilight walk down by the lake. Declan doesn't blink an eyelid.

When Sarah finds out I've given the dog away, she blows her top. All sorts of built-up shit and resentment comes blurting out. She's going off so badly that, hard as I try, I can't help but get hurt.

I scream, 'I want a divorce.'

'Don't you scream at me!' she screams. And she retreats into the house which we once shared.

After I calm down somewhat, I feel good. I obviously needed to state my truth. I want a divorce. I want to start a new life. I reflect on how helping out a mate ended up with me helping myself.

Two months later, Sarah moves out of the family home for good and I'm breathing again.

Declan is helping Tina heal. It turns out Tina's special brand of agoraphobia has another twist. Tina has discovered she can go out in the middle of the day if she takes Declan with her. Martin tells me if things keep going the way they are, Tina might soon be able to go out all by herself. Best of all, the trip to Europe has been postponed indefinitely and Martin has been able to drop down to three days a week at work.

We have our first gig today. Pistols in the Piano are back! A mate of Henry's is having her book launch at the local CWA hall. After the official bits, where apparently she is going to physically launch a free copy of her book from off of the stage and into the crowd, she wants the event to turn into a party. She asked if we could open our set with 'Paperback Writer' by the Beatles. We agreed. It has been such fun rehearsing the song, I reckon it will stay in our repertoire.

We have a guitarist now. See back in the 80s when we had Lip, he sang lead vocals but also played guitar. Now, we have Svetlana on vocals and, even though she plays the balalaika, it didn't quite work out when she brought it along to rehearsal one time. Fortuitously, I met this young bloke down at the Obsidian Tambourine while I was dropping off some herbs from my garden. His name is Seamus O'Reilly and he's a real whizz on the guitar. Plus, he has introduced us to some great songs from the more recent decades.

I'm down at the hall setting up my drum kit. Henry's playing Bach's Fugue in G minor with a big church organ sound from his keyboard set up. Svetlana pulls out some paper and a marker to write out the set lists. She's getting better but still mixes up her Russian and English alphabets. She writes something, she knows it's wrong and laughing out loud she shows Henry and me, Nanepback Pitep.

'Leave it,' says Henry. 'We can work that one out.'

Svetlana looks at me and I nod in agreement with Henry. 'It's Paperback Writer, easy!'

'No,' she says. 'It will not do.' She pulls out her mobile phone, which has an app to help her.

The more I get to know Svetlana, the more I like her. She is different, no doubt, but beyond all her Russian quirks is the real person: brutally honest, fiercely loyal and funny. Even funnier than Henry, I'm beginning to think.

Martin and Tina turn up. Martin is carrying his old Peavey amp and Tina has Martin's bass. It didn't register at first, but then I realise it's three in the arvo and Tina's out in broad daylight, and there's no Declan. Well, strike me blue. Who'd have thunk it!

'When is Seamus getting here?' asks Martin.

'He's doing lock up this afternoon at the café, so he can't get here till four thirty. We'll still have time for bit of a soundcheck. It'll all be fine. The launch doesn't start till five.'

'No worries, Smiddy. And by the way, I want to thank you. mate. Getting the band back together has been the best thing, eh?'

Henry pipes in. 'Bloody oath. Just like the old days. Well, not quite the same without Lip.'

Svetlana looks up at Henry.

'Actually, all things considered, it's even better now,' Henry backpedals.

'Slovo – ne vorobey, vyletit – ne poimayesh,' says Svetlana.

'So true, my dear, so true,' says Henry. He looks at the rest of us and translates. 'A spoken word is not a sparrow. Once it flies out, you can't catch it.'

Henry starts playing a Russian polka. Svetlana jumps up from the floor, all energy. She skips over to Tina and holds her arms out for a dance. The two women dance around the hall, laughing out loud.

Everything is good. The author turns up, and so do the caterers. Seamus turns up, sets up in a jiffy and we play 'Champagne Supernova' and 'Paperback Writer'. Tina stands at the back of the hall and gives feedback on sound levels.

I reckon twenty or thirty people max turn up for the launch. The author must be disappointed. Regardless, she steps up onto the stage and after thank yous and an explanation of what she is about to do, she turns her back and launches a copy of her book out into the hall. Nobody catches it. It hits the floor. A young boy of about eight swoops in and picks it up. 'I got it! I got it!' he calls out. The boy's mother mouths a sorry to the author. The author fakes a laugh. Henry steps up onto the stage and saves the situation. As arranged, Henry says a few things about the author and the book and how you can buy a copy. Then he does a reading.

He's a good old stick, Henry. It's so great to have him up here on the Central Coast. Credit for that has to go to Martin, Long Jetty's best salesperson. If Martin had his way, everyone we know would be living within walking distance from each other. Now that's the sort of travel Martin can agree to.

After the first set, which might I say went pretty well for our first gig, I find myself out the back with Martin. We are having a beer, a free beer thanks to the author.

'I've got a problem,' he says.

'Really?'

'Yep. Tina wants to do a big trip overseas. Can you believe it? She's wondering if you'd be able to take Declan back just while we're away.'

I stand there not knowing what to say. I finish off the beer.

Martin is waiting. 'Come on, help me, Smiddy.'

'I'm going to need some time, Martin. All I can think of at the moment is that we offload Declan to my daughter, she'll take him for sure, and then we all go on a band tour of Europe. We could even do a leg in Russia. Svetlana would have contacts there. We might even get free vodka while we're playing. We could even go by boat, if big old jet airliner exhaust is an issue.'

'Smiddy, I'm serious, man.'

'So am I,' I say with a wink. 'Has Tina started with the pleading? You know, like she did with getting a dog. Is she going, "Europe, Martin? Europe, Martin?"'

'Not yet, but it won't be long. Once she gets an idea…'

'OK. OK. Another wicked problem. You know me, I'll need time. And we better focus on our next set. That book launch crowd out there could cause merry hell if we don't perform up to scratch.'

We laugh.

'Hang on, Martin, I've got an idea. Sure, it's a band-aid solution, excuse the pun, but a temporary measure until we can sort this out good and proper. OK?'

Of course it is OK with Martin, he's been my mate for decades.

'When Tina starts up with the "Europe, Martin" business, just reply, "Dog, Tina."'

'Oh, Smiddy! You are a classic. Come on, let's go and play some tunes.'

IV. What is the antipodal point?

Lip, it's been a while, eh? Sure, we have the occasional exchange on Messenger. And you did come and visit last year before the big fellow died. But you were caught up with catching up. So many people to see.

The plan to do some songs together fell over pretty early in the piece. Maybe next time, Lip. When will that be?

You've been away a long while now, Henry.

It takes a certain kind of person to be able to live in a desert. The sun and the dust, the lack of plants, cloudless skies and no busy streets. A dog is a good idea. Air conditioning a must, especially in a donga. No need for doonas.

Lip liked the solitude. He could write poems and songs and draw naked women. He could crack a beer at nine thirty, or earlier. The job was seven days a week, but easy as piss. One drive around the boundary fence in the morning and once again in the afternoon. Push, pull or swipe off any electrocuted animals with the special non-conductive pole, and write up any needed repairs.

The battering ram thumped from seven thirty to four thirty. Lip timed it. Tempo: twenty six booms per minute. A back beat to life. Not so welcome in the morning after a big night at the titty bar. But otherwise, the perfect metronome.

BOOM... BOOM... BOOM...

Last Saturday I got going on this story, a task sent to me by Lip. Write a story based on the photo of him, in the desert, with a dog. He thinks he looks like Mel Gibson, I think he looks like David Essex. What I notice most in the photo is his shirt. A red checked short sleeve number. The sleeves are virtually non existent. They are like small eaves for the upper arm. This was a style for a while. A style that Lip liked very much. He had several T-shirts with poor excuses for sleeves.

The story so far, exists only as a journal entry. One day it will be assigned its very own file and be one step closer towards being published on my blog, or chucked into some random collection of short stories that I'll try to flog to a real publisher. Or maybe it will sit in the computer, never to be used for anything.

So this is how it is now. Occasional dabbles, waiting for the next big push.

Lip inserted his own beats in between booms.

BOOM chuckawucka, BOOM chuckawucka…was a common morning rhythm. Simple, slow, went well with coffee. When the caffeine did hit, he would add in an extra wucka. BOOM chuckawuckawucka BOOM…things picking up now.

Get in the ute and do a lap of the boundary. Where's that China Crisis cassette?

One morning, after a big night at the titty bar, Lip dressed up in the clothes left behind by the girl who rooted like a demon. How she got back into town with no clothes and no car was one of those mysteries never to be solved. She just up and left at seven thirty three, holding her head and cursing the battering ram. She left a cotton blouse, a denim skirt and a pair of brown leather boots.

BOOM diddly squiddly widdly BOOM kick up some dust with the cowgirl boots. Twirl around, get that skirt lifting, reveal man bits to the world of the desert. No one watching. Camp it up, Lip.

Was she wearing undies? Can't find them anywhere in the donga. She definitely wasn't wearing any when she took off, howling like a banshee. Can't recall how I picked her up. Do remember her tongue in my ear as I drove her back here.

Lip looked at himself in girl's clobber. It's a lark, bloody hilarious, the boys back east would love it.

He waltzed, BOOM tick tick BOOM tick tick BOOM…

That same morning Lip found a big hole in the fence. So big, he could drive the ute through it. That was probably how the hole was made. Some rum soaked yahoos from town probably smashed through to find some gems. Apparently, so the titty bar gossip went, the battering ram sent sapphires and rubies flying a hundred metres or more. No wonder the fence was electrified.

Lip was not allowed inside the perimeter. His donga was on the outside. 'Just clear off the wildlife and report any damage. Nothing else, OK?' were the instructions on day one.

The temptation was too great. Being dressed as a cowgirl, and the raging hangover, only made the idea so much more plausible. Lip drove inside the compound.

I'll stay out of sight. Park just this side of the rise. Have a sneaky look around. A gem or two would be a nice reward for my loyal service to the company.

Down in the dust on his belly, Lip crawled up the rise to survey the scene. The battering ram was massive. There were some buildings around it and some parked cars, they looked tiny in comparison.

BOOM ruby ruby ruby, BOOM…

There was no one in sight. The workers would be busy, or not busy, and hanging in the air conditioning. Drinking coffee. Talking shit.

Lip stood up bold as brass and walked down towards the operation. He saw the conveyor belt delivering rock to the ram.

BOOM crunch, BOOM crunch, BOOM…dust and rock fragments exploded outwards. Parabolic arcs sprayed the surrounding desert floor. An oversized bulldozer pushed the debris into piles.

The driver won't be looking out for men in drag looking for a bit of bling.

Lip pushed on.

The gossip was correct. At about a hundred metres out, sun-lit flashes of blue and red twinkled on the ground. Lip picked up some rocks with the glint. He had nothing to carry them in. The cotton blouse had no pockets. The denim skirt likewise. The boots were made for walking and scooting.

The giant bulldozer turned and headed straight for Lip.

Grab what you can, boy. And get the fuck out of here.

Lip drove out of the hole in the fence and planned to burn the clothes.

They'll be looking for a girl. I'll bury the rocks under the dog kennel. There's no way Patch will let anyone scratch around there.

The company's security division arrived the next day. They turned the donga upside down and inside out. They didn't find any gems. But one officer, with a smile on his dial that Lip felt deserved a punching, said, 'What have we here?' He held aloft on the end of a Biro a pair of women's panties. All black lace and snail trail.

Lip, Please find the story attached. Is that when you headed overseas, Lip? After that job in Port Hedland?

You went to the northern hemisphere, I went a hundred ks north of Sydney. You international, me regional. Both of us succumbing to society's call: grow up, settle down, make something of yourself. Both of us fucking up. Now we chat online and wonder what to do next. Is there enough time for something 'next'. Do you like the story?

I know it's cold over there, and you've told me how you miss home. You like the heat.

There's a great op-shop around the corner from my place. Come over and we can choose some clothes to wear now we've got the band back on the road. You might even find a shirt with those silly cut-back sleeves, Henry.

Last Night

1 November 2019

The yelling starts about two a.m. and wakes us both up. It's not unusual to wake at this time, bladders make sure of that. But you accept bladders. Loud angry men is a different story. It's not even Saturday night, so what is all this yelling about?

Out there, in the yelling department, one man in particular is holding court. The others voices are lesser. They sound like they're trying to tell the main yeller to shut up. We can't work out the words being shouted, except for the occasional 'Fuck!' 'Fuck' cuts through. It's the anger, though, that is most disturbing.

We both turn on our opposite sides and rearrange sheets and blankets and pillows and snuggle down. It will stop soon, we think. We haven't spoken yet. We know what each other is thinking and what state of slumber we are in. Sleep with someone every night for an extended period and you don't need to discuss these things, they are known, information exchanged by nocturnal osmosis, incubated in the warmth of human proximity and contact. Comforting.

Silence returns. We shuffle a bit more, snuggle down further. The angry man must have moved on. Just a small Thursday night aberration. Tomorrow's Friday; everything's fine on Fridays. Nothing, not even a shitstorm at work, can wreck Fridays. We feel ourselves and each other falling, sinking, drifting, transitioning into slumber. Warm feet touch.

He starts up again. This is ridiculous. He's on his own now, shouting at no one, shouting at the moon maybe. It goes on and on. Again, words indiscernible. The anger palpable, clogging the clear night air, disturbing those in bed, like us. We shift around. Still no speaking required, an understanding that there is nothing to be done at this point, except attempting to shut him out, to exercise control over our own minds, to beat him by being unperturbed – able to sleep no matter what filth and disgust and insanity he spews into our neighbourhood.

It goes on.

We both wonder about the durability of his vocal chords. Surely, they must wear out soon. Or soon he will feel better from all that venting, surely. We wonder why the police haven't arrived. Someone must have called the police. We haven't called the police. Oh yeah, everyone else woken by the angry man must be thinking the same. Someone will have called the police. They will be here soon. Surely.

I've had enough. 'I'm going out for a look,' I say.

'Don't approach him,' you say with that special loving concern you have for all creatures, including me. Especially me.

'Don't worry,' I say with a sense of self-preservation that I chiefly credit to you. Without you, I'd be charging down there naked and stumbling into all sorts of strife. 'I'm just going to see where he is so I can call the police and tell them where to head.' I put on a T-shirt and shorts.

You get up and put on that fluffy white robe. We walk out the front together. We have forgotten about the bindi-eyes. We support each other as we swipe the little pricks off our bare feet.

'There's a group of people down at the Metro on the corner, I think they're talking with him,' I say.

The yelling has stopped.

We go back inside and into bed. With a bit of luck, we won't need to call the police. We nestle into each other. Waiting. Hoping.

No yelling.

The group of people from down at the Metro are walking up past our place. We sit up in bed and look out onto the street. The glow from their mobile phones illuminates their faces. Two young men and three young women. It must be three a.m. by now. The young people walk and post and talk quietly to each other. So considerate.

Without saying a word, we thank the young people and turn on our sides.

Now, sleep.

Look at Those Idiots

It's afternoon now. The stillness and promise of morning gone for the day. The wind is blowing in from the north-east. White horses appear and disappear on the blue ocean. Beach sand being redistributed, wiping out footprints.

She's in her fifties now. Grey hairs appear and then are disappeared with the help of a two-part solution. The lines on her face and neck are going nowhere. Daily walks add to the pull of gravity on muscle and bone. The beauty and optimism of youth, gone forever now.

Picture this: she is on the watching platform down by the beach, watching a family of four, an uncomplicated family of four: father, mother, son and daughter. She estimates the father to be thirty-seven and two years older than the wife. Likewise, the son is two years older than his sister, who looks eight.

She guesses they have driven for thirty hot and traffic-congested minutes from, say, Watanobbi? The kids have pestered the parents to go to the beach. The father wanted to sit home and drink beer after another unfulfilling day at work. The mother has thawed meat and washed the salad vegetables for the family dinner, and she still has clothes on the line to bring in. The kids got their way.

The family walk onto the beach and head towards the flags. They lean into the headwind, sand is whipping their bare legs. The boy is out front, leading the way. His boogie board is flapping wildly, barely controllable. The mother walks next to the daughter with one hand on her shoulder. The young girl is crying from the sting of the windblown sand. The father is at the rear, an umbrella tucked under an arm, an esky in one hand, and two folded beach chairs in his other hand. His hat blows off.

'Look at those idiots,' she says to herself. 'They should've been here in the morning. It was beautiful this morning. What do people expect – coming to the beach at this time of the day in summer?

The café under the surf club is closing up for the day. This morning the café was packed. You couldn't get a table. She wanted to sit and watch the glittering ocean, and watch the regulars. There's one group in particular that she has noticed. They're there every day. Six of them. Three men and three women. They must be couples but it's impossible to know who is with who. They sit in different arrangements each day and the men talk with the men and the women talk with the women. They're older than she. She figures, late sixties or early seventies. This in itself is nothing of great interest, but what does grab her attention is the large green wine bottle, filled with what she assumes is water, the large jar of Vegemite and the large tub of margarine. The same every morning.

Somehow, her timing has never been quite right, she has never seen any one of the six touch any of these three items. The bottle just sits there, the Vegemite jar as well, and the margarine tub is always open with a knife stuck in it. By the time she gets there, they are all talking and the plates, cups and glasses that also sit on the table are all finished with. She assumes one or more of the group drink water from the bottle with the coffees that they have ordered and paid for, and that one or more of them order toast or a breakfast muffin and apply their own spread. Perhaps some of them order other food, but she doesn't know. She can only assume. She can't get down earlier to see what happens when this group arrive and set up, and order, and eat, because she waits for her husband to leave for work before she heads off for her morning walk to the beach. She assumes that is her duty as a stay-at-home wife.

The family have finished setting up their little camp on the beach. The mother is putting sunscreen on the daughter, the boy is already in the water paddling about on his boogie board. The father, who did manage to get his hat back, is sitting on one of the beach chairs, taking in the scene. The umbrella is stuck in the sand, but hasn't been opened. It would be blown away for sure. A gust would uproot it and send it cartwheeling along the beach, threatening to spear someone on its way. The father would have to chase it down, apologising to people on the run. The mother would be watching with her hands to her mouth, hoping that no one gets hurt, the daughter would be screaming, the boy out in the water would be oblivious. It will only be a matter of time, she thinks, before the boy gets stung by a bluebottle. The lifeguard will attend, and point out the yellow warning sign as he sprays on the vinegar. And the onlookers, including herself, will be thinking, 'Look at those idiots.'

But the umbrella wasn't opened, was it? And being down closer to the water where the sand is wet and unable to be lifted and swept across the contours of the beach, the family look comfortable and happy. The daughter has gone down to the water's edge and is running back and forth with the small waves that wash up and down the sloping shoreline. The mother goes to the esky and pulls out two stubbies of beer. She sits down next to her husband. They clink the necks of their bottles. The boy catches a wave and somehow, so far, has avoided the stingers.

She has all the time in the world to watch this family. Her husband, who she waved goodbye to this morning, won't be home till way after she has gone to bed. He texted earlier to say he has been held up, as per usual, with all this new reporting and accountability that must be attended to. He'll grab a bite to eat and have it at his desk. Don't wait up, he texted. She assumes he is having an affair. It's happened before and she was surprised how little it bothered her. She has the brand-new home with ocean views, she doesn't have to work, she's never had to work, and she walks twice a day down to the beach, where she never swims. She watches people and imagines all their unhappiness and anxieties. On a good day, she'll witness an argument between a couple, or someone unable to start their car.

She never had children. And when she sees these horrible things at the supermarket, giving merry hell to their mothers, she smiles inside. Her trolley isn't overloaded and she isn't in a rush. She doesn't have to hunt out the specials. She can afford whatever she likes.

This morning when she watched the three couples at the table adorned with the green bottle, and the jar of Vegemite, and the tub of margarine, she was certain there was a tension in the air. The way that one woman spoke to one of the other women was quite telling, she thought. She assumed that most people would conclude that this was a group of great friends who delight in their regular morning meetings at the café down by the beautiful beachside. But she knows better. The men's laughter at each other's jokes and anecdotes is clearly faked jocularity. The women, all wearing clothes from the same factory outlet over at Tuggerah, appear to be unified in their uniforms, but really they are too terrified to look any different from each other. They are, all of them, fearful conformists. Every muscle straining to maintain the appearance of harmony and contentment.

One of them owns that stupid repurposed bottle, she thought. One day I'll witness one of them picking it up and smashing it on the concourse, or better still, smashing it on someone's head.

Picture this: to the south, the sky has darkened. She, who has been watching the family, waiting for some drama, smiles. She is happy she waited, even though the varicose veins in her calves are throbbing. Some people on the beach have spotted the oncoming storm and are making their way back to the car park. They are not idiots, they know that a late afternoon summer storm can bring havoc, and hail. Cars need to be safely under cover. The happy family on the beach appear oblivious. The father is now in the water with his son. He is launching him onto waves. The mother is building a sandcastle with her daughter.

Lightning bolts hit the sea way out near the horizon, so far away you can't hear them. The nor'-easter begins to abate.

She decides against leaving; she has to see what happens when the storm hits and these idiots are caught out.

The wind dies off completely. It is still now, and the sky is green and grey. The man and his son come out of the water and stand, looking out at the lightning. The mother leaves her daughter by the water's edge and goes to get towels for the boys.

The southerly hits. The family run back to their camp. They pick up their gear and start to make their way back to the car park. Large sporadic drops of rain begin. You can hear thunder now. Soon, it will be a downpour. But she waits on the platform and watches. This is good, this is how the world works, she thinks. Don't people get it?

The rain increases, the family run faster. She smiles. Idiots get what they deserve.

As the family of four get closer, she sees that they are laughing. The father is laughing. The mother is laughing. The boy and the girl are laughing. Hysterically laughing, all of them. The temperature has dropped at least ten degrees and they are wet, and they are laughing.

She turns and walks away from the beach. She is wet, and so angry she starts to cry.

Shepherd's Warning
9 December 2019

We were told to stay indoors. That worked for a day or two and then the smoke inside was just as bad as outside. So we go outside now. The UV radiation levels are down, no need for sunscreen.

We've taken up smoking again, thirty-four cigarettes a day, we are told. No cost, no butts.

You can see the asbestos fibres rising off the super six roofing. We used to cut that stuff with angle grinders, no masks, no goggles, no earmuffs. The good old days.

The shrubs and trees are flowering magnificently. Best it's been for years. And the mango trees are fruiting. Love mangoes in summer.

A new decade is about to begin. We will call it the 20s. We will see the population hit eight billion. We will keep revising the number of degrees Celsius that the world has warmed. We will celebrate births. We will argue politics and religion until the cows come home.

The cows are coming.

Op-shopping Across the Universe

My girlfriend is an alien, and I love her dearly. She is the best thing that has ever happened to me. She is kind, non-judgemental, has six nipples and can breathe underwater. We have lots of fun in the bedroom and at the beach. But our favourite pastime together is op-shopping.

Her name is Lakshmi.

I say, lucky me.

I met Lakshmi in Nambour, Queensland, eight years ago. Every couple have their 'How did you two get together?' story, and ours is a pretty good one. Not that we can tell anyone about it. But it's our story and that's all that matters.

If you've ever been to Nambour, you may know it as the place where Kevin Rudd and Wayne Swan went to high school. And if you haven't been there, it's one of those towns which had the life sucked out of it after some heartless corporation built a massive shopping centre on a nearby swamp. That's Nambour. And another thing you may or may not know is that Nambour floods real easy.

So, on this particular day, the start of the 'me and Lakshmi' story, it was pissing down like I'd never seen before and Petrie Creek was breaking its bank. Pretty soon, a whole bunch of us were stuck inside the Neighbours Aid Community Store on Howard Street.

Most of us who were stuck there that day were genuine op-shoppers. In addition, there were a couple of Aldi shoppers who ducked in for shelter, and there was this one dude who I don't know where he came from, but he started causing a bit of a commotion. He could've been on ice, he could've been born that way, but what was certain was that he was angry and loud, psychotic and perilous. I was amongst the second-hand books when I first heard his ranting. I moved towards the front counter, where he was causing the commotion, and I noticed Lakshmi in the section with all the bric-a-brac. I had spotted Lakshmi a few times before; her multicoloured hair was hard to miss.

Everyone was looking at the mad man. Everyone except Lakshmi, who seemed oblivious as she picked up and examined various items from the shelves and tables.

The psycho man was yelling, 'This place is fucked,' over and over. He paced around in circles of ever increasing radius.

People nearby were stepping back.

He bumped into a table covered with doonas and blankets and swiped them all off. 'This place is fucked.' Then he wheeled around and crashed into the front counter.

There were two elderly ladies serving behind the counter. They stepped back as far as they could, backs against the wall, and watched in fear as the man now started swiping items off the counter.

'Fuck!'

Off went the sign explaining how all items presented for sale must have a price tag.

'Fuck!'

Off went the charity tin for loose change.

'This place is fucked!' he screamed as he swiped off a pile of books that someone had obviously left there while they continued on shopping in some other section.

He hollered again as he sent a glass-topped display tray, filled with dead people's jewellery, frisbeeing across the room. A large man wearing a hi-vis vest, who had come from the sorting room out the back in response to all the commotion, just managed to side-step the twirling tray. He could have been chopped off at the knees.

The only thing left on the counter now was the cash register. We all saw it. It would be next to go. It was large and metal and heavy. I looked over to the large man who had just dodged the jewellery tray. So did a few others. We assumed if this situation was anyone's responsibility, he was the most likely candidate. He saw us all looking at him and his shoulders shrank and his face went pale. There was a moment of stillness. I looked back at the crazy man, he was also looking at the man in the vest and he started laughing. Maniacal laughing. The man in the vest started shaking and fumbled a mobile phone out of his pocket. The lunatic turned back and looked at the register. Everyone knew what was going to happen. I could hear people sucking in air and whispering Oh no's.

Full of adrenalin, like everyone else, I stepped forward into the circle of danger, unlike anyone else. 'Hey,' I yelled just as he was grabbing onto the sides of the register.

The crazed man turned around and looked my way. He bared his teeth and started panting.

'It's OK, man. Just settle down. Everything will be OK,' I said. Lame, I know. And it didn't work, not one iota.

'Fuck off!' He turned back to the register.

This was when Lakshmi stepped in. She walked right up to the man and put her hand on his back between his shoulders. He turned around and looked at her. Her hair glowed. Her eyes penetrated into his scrambled mind. He calmed for a moment, and then a look of fear came across his face.

At this point, I heard a high-pitched sound. The man put his hands over his ears and stepped back. He started whimpering.

'Go for a swim,' sang Lakshmi. Her hair was waving like the ocean and shimmering in shades of green and blue. 'The water. The lovely water.'

Lakshmi's singing had a calming effect on us all. The danger had subsided. The wild erratic drug-fucked pyscho fell to his knees and sobbed.

'Go to the water. The healing water. The water.' Her musical voice lifted the man off his knees and walked him to the door and out into the flashing flood.

When the flood subsided, no one who was in the op-shop that day could describe to the police, or later to friends and family, exactly what had really happened. Everyone had a slightly different version, and the one I have just recounted is simply mine. It was magical and weird. Lakshmi's hair and her voice were definitely something from out of this world. No one cared. We were grateful and in awe of her amazing feat. Calming the beast.

My car was ruined by the flood. As I watched it being towed away, I felt a hand placed on my back. I turned around, it was Lakshmi. She smiled and led me to her spaceship disguised as a car. We have been together ever since.

Lakshmi's actions at the op-shop in Nambour had drawn some attention. Worst of all, the mad man who she sent into the flood waters later reappeared as a born-again Christian preaching on the streets. One day down at the Mooloolaba Esplanade, Lakshmi and I were enjoying an after-swim gelato and the mad man spotted us. He pointed at Lakshmi and started ranting about the devil incarnate. Things became too hot for an alien in Queensland. We headed south.

We chose Long Jetty because of the wide choice of nearby sleeping locations for Lakshmi. Most nights she sleeps with me in our queen-size futon, but, once or twice a week, Lakshmi needs to sleep under water. Under the jetty is a good place and an easy walk from our two-bedroom cottage. She jokes about how the seaweed caresses her skin and how the crabs do a phenomenal job trimming her hair. Occasionally, she'll sleep in Toowoon Bay, where there's not too much surf. After a night in the ocean, Lakshmi is rejuvenated to the point of literally bouncing out of her cute alien skin.

'It's the synergistic effect of the iodine, whale urine and dissolved oxygen,' she claims.

How can I argue? Even though I did both Bio and Chem at school, the nutritional and metabolic realities of creatures from Juno are areas of knowledge way beyond my tiny human capacities.

Yes, Lakshmi comes from a planet called Juno. She can't live there because of overpopulation. Every year, the planet's government conduct a ballot of all five-year-old children and draw out the names of who will be required to emigrate. When Lakshmi told me this, I instinctively felt sorry for her. She laughed at my concern and explained that to be chosen was a big privilege on Juno. She explained how when a family has a child drawn from the ballot there is great celebration in the local community. The child is educated in a special school in the city. No expenses are spared to set up the family and the child with all the very best technology. Lakshmi's spaceship, for example, which is cleverly disguised as a Subaru Liberty, is a wonder of wonders. It can fly in the sky and dive under the oceans. It can even disappear from sight. Inside, in the wagon section, is a doorway to a virtual Juno, where Lakshmi can visit her family and favourite places on her home planet. And in the centre console there is a teleporter through which she exchanges op-shop treasures for gold. Juno, Lakshmi tells me, is a planet formed from a sixth-generation supernova and gold is as common as dirt. Rubies are also common but, unlike gold, they are hard to sell on Earth without attracting too much attention.

On Juno, as here on Earth, everyone has to earn a living. Fortuitously, the people back on Juno are absolutely mad about the stuff we don't want any more and end up dumping into charity bins. Lakshmi's business is thriving. Lakshmi, out of the kindness of her 250-bpm heart, has employed me to write descriptions of the stuff she sends back home. She tells me that her goods are attracting even greater attention back on Juno since my authentic native descriptions of the items and their cultural value have been included in the packaging.

And here's an interesting fact. The first time Lakshmi exported op-shop stuff from Earth back to Juno, she wrapped everything in bubble wrap. Nothing like bubble wrap existed on Juno at that time and it caused a sensation. It was lauded as one of the greatest inventions of all time. Without bubble wrap, the postage and packaging services on Juno were notorious for breakages. This planet that could invent invisible rocket ships and control its population without mass revolt was hopeless at protecting goods in transit. Hard to believe, isn't it? But I will tell you something: Lakshmi never lies.

One of my hobbies is songwriting. I compose on an old Roland Juno-106 synthesiser. I picked it up from an op-shop in Newtown, Sydney, long before I met Lakshmi, the girl from Juno. If I was superstitious, I suppose I could claim that this coincidence was not a coincidence at all, and that the purchase of the Juno was an omen for my future encounter with an alien from a planet of the same name. But that is beside the point, the point being that Lakshmi is brutally honest. When I play her my songs, she listens without any bias or favouritism. She has a ratings scale – Gold is poor, Ruby is mediocre, Whale Piss is good, and Bubble Wrap is hit material. She does occasionally score one of my songs a Gold. It hurts a bit, but I get over it and really appreciate the honest feedback.

I have compiled a playlist of my songs that have been given the Bubble Wrap thumbs-up from Lakshmi. It's available on SoundCloud and I'm getting more likes than ever. Life is good. My desire to be a rich and famous songwriter died long ago. After years of playing in bands and trying in vain to get publishing deals and recording contracts, I now only write music for the sake of a good song and the joy I get from the creative process. With the help of Lakshmi's great ear, I now have the additional joy of knowing that others are enjoying my songs. It's all I need.

I'm waiting for Lakshmi to come home from sleeping under the jetty. I've made us bowls of muesli with banana on top. Lakshmi loves bananas; so do I. She is late, which is unusual. The bananas are going brown. At least I held off adding the milk. Where is she?

A helicopter flies above and a siren is getting louder. I walk out the front door and look down the street towards the lake. I can't see anything of concern and the helicopter moves off. The siren drops in frequency as it passes by, heading somewhere else.

Today, we are heading out to Dubbo. There's a Red Cross and a Smith Family shop there. Country op-shops are great, and so are country people. Lakshmi can buy some stuff and I'll get some stories for my part of the business. We'll do our work, if you can call it that, then visit the zoo. Lakshmi hasn't seen a giraffe before. We'll fly there in the Subaru Liberty, which will be switched to invisible.

Where is she? We'd better get going.

I walk down to the lake shore. There are three people standing out at the end of the jetty, right above where Lakshmi sleeps. I step up my pace. There is a young boy all excited and telling an adult couple what he has discovered.

'It's a lady, she's lying on the bottom in the weed. Get down and look underneath!'

The couple are obviously dubious. And they don't want to lie down on the warped hardwood boards covered in shag shit. I arrive and the boy implores me to have a look.

'Sure,' I say. I lie down and see Lakshmi asleep on the bottom. She has overslept. Unusual, but it has happened before, though never this late!

I stand back up. 'It's a manikin,' I say. 'Someone's dumped it here as a joke. I'll call the council and they can get someone to come and get it out.'

'No, it's not,' says the boy. He lies down and looks again. 'She's real! Look, look. A crab is eating her hair.' He jumps back up. He grabs his fishing rod and backpack. 'I'm going home to call the police. That's not a manikin. It's a dead body.' He runs off.

The couple look at me.

'It's a manikin. You know what kids are like.'

The couple walk away.

I have to act, now. I wait until the couple are far enough away. I slide down into the water. It's cold and my feet hit the muddy bottom. I duck under the jetty and reach down and grab Lakshmi's arm. Instinctively, she grabs onto me and pulls me under. I scream and struggle, all my oxygen lost in bubbles.

Lakshmi wakes up and realises it's me. We surface. I'm gasping for air, she is horrified at her actions.

'I'm so sorry. Are you OK?' She holds me, warms me.

'What happened? You never sleep this late. A boy has spotted you. He's going home to call the police. He thinks you're a dead body. We've got to get home.'

We climb back onto the jetty and head home. There are early walkers and bike riders out on the lakeside track. We are getting lots of looks.

In our street, everything is quiet. No nosey neighbours peeking out at the man with his alien girlfriend sneaking home wet and guilty-looking, I think.

We dry off and eat our muesli.

Lakshmi is worried. 'I don't want to move again,' she says. 'I like it here. I like it here with you.'

'We can stay. I'm sure no one will cause us any trouble.'

'It's not trouble for you. It's me who doesn't belong in this world.'

'If it's trouble for you, Lakshmi, it's trouble for me. And who says you don't belong here? People love you. It shouldn't matter what planet you were born on.'

'You are so kind.' Lakshmi hugs me tight and kisses me with her banana-flavoured mouth.

I feel the special tingle which always accompanies her out-of-this-world touch.

We decide it would be a good distraction from our worries to just get on with our plan. The Subaru Liberty glides over the Great Dividing Range. I'm wearing polarised sunglasses and watching sapphire blue light reflecting off the creeks and dams. Up here in the spaceship we are invisible, safe.

We land outside Dubbo and with a flick of a switch the car-cum-spaceship becomes visible again. In town, some people gawk at Lakshmi's newly trimmed multicoloured hair. Out here, they just think she is some city hipster. And really, she doesn't draw too much attention back in Long Jetty either. I'm sure some of the café crowd down there assume that the tall thin girl with the outrageous op-shop wardrobe is a leftover from the days when the Jetty was a low-rent fibro haven for junkies on the methadone program.

'Everything's going to be OK,' I reassure Lakshmi.

We lose ourselves in the Red Cross shop. I go one way and Lakshmi the other. We cross paths several times and touch hands. It's a good store, not too organised, little nooks and crannies with unexpected gems. I pick up a few LP records that I once owned back when I was a teenager and a really cool framed print of a storm at sea. Lakshmi finds a hula-hula figurine, a plate with a fish on it, and a green glass liquor decanter. From a $20 note, we get $1.50 change, which Lakshmi inserts into the slot on the head of a plastic guide dog that sits next to the counter.

We do the Smith Family shop as well. Lakshmi buys some ugg boots.

'You do know it's coming into summer?' I ask.

'I'm hungry. Let's get some lunch,' she says.

My stomach drops. Something is going on. I know it. I know it in the tone of her voice and the look on her gorgeous face, the face I fell in love with eight years ago when she drove me home after my car was destroyed by a flash flood. She is exotic on a universal level – her planet and galaxy at the other end of the 5th Great Wormhole. Sometimes, I try to visualise Lakshmi's op-shop exports shooting timelessly along the wormhole all the way to planet Juno. It's all a little too much for my parochial Milky Way head. But Lakshmi isn't too much for me. She is simple and real in a way that engulfs me and my human heart. I ache when she aches.

'Two salad rolls, please,' I order from a classic little Asian-looking woman in a classic little sandwich shop in the main street of Dubbo. It's classic, not retro, because the shop hasn't changed in forty years or more.

'Would you like some chilli on your salad rolls, love?' The woman serving sounds just as Aussie and just as country as the op-shop ladies, who definitely weren't of Asian appearance. I guess you'd call them of Anglo appearance, but we don't do that. Anglo is the default. Everything other than a white Caucasian look gets some label of appearance. I look at Lakshmi, the girl from Juno. She is beautiful beyond appearance.

Like we all are, if we could only see by not seeing what's merely on the surface.

Woman, lady, girl. Man, bloke, boy. Asian, Anglo, African, Aboriginal. Black, brown, yellow, white. Gay, straight, queer, cis. Human, alien. All just words, belying the fragile sentient beings to which they are attached. The universe observing itself with trillions of eyes and falling short when it comes to the utterance of words from mouths.

There is a glass cabinet with sponge cakes, rock cakes, Neenish tarts, custard tarts, Chelsea buns, finger buns, vanilla slices, apple slices, plain scones, date scones, fruit mince pies and loganberry pies. Timeless, comforting. This shop, a small oasis of constancy in a world changing every day. No, every minute.

I think about our little home back in Long Jetty filled with all the old stuff we have found from op-shops all over Australia. Lakshmi and me curled up together, under a crocheted woollen blanket, in front of the gas heater, listening to LPs at thirty-three and one-third revolutions per minute. Our sanctuary, one small eddy in the swirl of the cosmos. Our place, our niche. I fear the worst.

We drive over to the botanical gardens. We take our salad rolls and the cakes and drinks we chose. We find a bench in the Japanese garden that overlooks the koi carp pond. The sun is warm.

We eat our lunch in between some small talk about the lovely day, the lovely park and the lovely people who served us. I watch Lakshmi wash down her rock cake with a swig of ginger beer. I sense we won't be seeing any giraffe today. She turns and looks at me. Here it comes.

The boy on the jetty will not forget what he saw this morning. Neither will the early morning walkers who saw two dripping wet creatures scurrying away from the lake. And though I didn't spot any neighbours as we slipped into our home, there is always someone who sees.

'We have to move, don't we?' I say.

'It's all going to start up again. The word is out. There's a freak in town. You know the gig. Nambour all over again.' Lakshmi looks down in her lap.

I can smell her tears. I can hear the hum of her sadness. 'Well, you know, it ain't that bad. A new start? A change is as good as a holiday, so they say.' I don't want to leave Long Jetty either, but I put some spin on it. Poor Lakshmi.

'I will go by myself. It's not fair on you.'

'No way. I'm coming. You can't get rid of me that easy.'

Lakshmi slides across the bench and wraps herself around me. 'I love you,' she sings into my ear.

Lakshmi left three weeks ago, the day after she slept in under the jetty. The day after our salad rolls by the koi pond. It turned out that the Smith Family ugg boots she purchased in Dubbo were in preparation for her next op-shopping adventure: Russia! Much as I begged Lakshmi to take me with her, it didn't happen. She argued that I'd miss swimming at the beach, whereas in a cold climate, she would be able to hide under furs and be less obviously alien. And then she spoke to me in fluent Russian, something which I had no idea about up until that point. She told me how she studied English and Russian at her special school after she'd been selected for emigration in the ballot and assigned Earth as her destination. She said that my lack of the language would draw too much unwanted attention.

On our last night together, she slept in our bed. We entwined from sunset till dawn. We cried and we laughed, and played in our special intergalactic way. She insisted I find another girl, an Earthling this time. She said I should forget her and move on. Yeah, right.

The mob with pitchforks and flaming torches turned up just after dark on the day Lakshmi disappeared over the northern horizon in her flying Subaru. They assembled on the paved area out the front of what was once our home, now just a house, not a home at all. The boy from the jetty was standing in the front. His parents behind him on either side.

A middle-aged man dressed in lycra, who was wearing a cycling helmet with a flashing LED on top of his angry head, stepped out from the mob. 'We want the witch!' He punched the air.

The mob echoed, 'We want the witch! We want the witch!'

'Go away! Leave me alone, please. Just leave me alone,' I pleaded. I was still deeply disturbed by having to farewell Lakshmi only hours before.

The father of the boy asked his son while pointing at me, 'That's him, isn't it?'

'Yes, it's him.'

Then another person stepped forward. It was Lynette, the red-haired lady with the cranky face who lived directly across the road from me. She had a security camera above her front door and bars on every window. She'd only ever spoken to me once. It was to tell me that if I didn't take my bins back in after garbage day she would phone council and I would get a fine.

'Where is she?' she demanded. 'We've been watching you and your freak. This is a good neighbourhood. There are children living in this street, you know!'

'There is no one here but me. Now go away or I'll call the police.'

'Go on, call them. We've already reported her,' said the bicycle man.

The mob started up again, 'We want the witch! We want the witch!'

I pulled out my mobile phone and started filming what was going on. Lynette screamed at me to stop. Then a young man who I'd never seen before, came from out of nowhere and punched me in the face. I dropped to the floor of my front porch. Dazed, I felt the mob trampling over the top of me as they poured into the house. Blood was flowing out of my nose, I could taste the iron.

I was scrambling around the porch trying to find my mobile phone when I heard a voice.

'I've called the cops.' It was Martin, my next-door neighbour. He was out on the street.

Tina his wife stood by his side. 'Bloody mongrels,' I heard her say.

I stood up, a bit dizzy, and staggered over to join my neighbours out on the street. I looked back at what was once my home with Lakshmi.

'She left this morning, didn't she?' Somehow, Tina knew.

We could hear banging and crashing inside the house and someone called out, 'She's not here!'

Sirens came into hearing. The mob began spewing out the front door and onto the street. I spotted the young fellow that had clocked me before and I stuck out my foot and tripped him good and proper. He hit the asphalt hard.

'That'd be right! Run away, Lynette!' Martin yelled to our red-headed neighbour. 'Hope you choke on your stupid Australian flag, ya bigot!'

Flashing blue lights illuminated the dispersing mob. The police nabbed the parents of the boy who started all the hysteria and the bloke I had tripped. After speaking to Martin and Tina and me, the police went over for a talk with Lynette. Later, they asked if I wanted to press charges. I said no. They indicated that they would likely pursue the matter further. Affray, home invasion, assault, they mentioned.

The police took photos and left. Martin and Tina invited me to stay in the spare room at their place. I declined.

Three weeks is a long time alone. The agreement is that we won't contact each other for six months. 'Let some water pass under the jetty,' said Lakshmi.

Thankfully, the mob haven't come back. My battered faith in humanity has been somewhat restored by offers of assistance from some of the decent folk who live around the area. I've gotten to know Martin and Tina much better. I never knew, but Lakshmi talked to them often when I was not home. They both loved her friendship and her zany wit. The police have laid some charges and let me know I may be called as a witness. Whatever.

I'm having a bowl of muesli with banana on top. The hula-hula figurine sits in front of me on the dining table. It will go on the dashboard of the car I must soon buy. It was Lakshmi's parting op-shop gift to me. Exotic, playful. I wonder how cold it is in Russia.

I hear someone on the front porch and then a knock. I open the door to find a man holding a parcel which I have to electronically sign for on a hand held device. The parcel is the size and shape of an LP record, but thicker. There is some strange foreign lettering on a label: почта России.

Looks Russian to me.

My pulse quickens.

Back inside, I tear open the packaging. I can smell Lakshmi's touch. Inside is a vinyl LP box set titled *Learn Russian in Record Time*, and a fur lined cap with ear flaps.

Human hormones rush my system and the world changes colour.

Is there a note? I look through the packaging and find it. In her unmistakable handwriting:

Six months? Stupid, stupid, stupid. You get six weeks. Start learning! I'll pick you up in my lime-green Lad Vesta. It goes like a rocket.

Lakshmi.

Lucky me.

I Heard the News Today, Oh Boy!
20 December 2019

Australia is burning and POTUS has been impeached. It doesn't matter what our PM says about reaching our Paris commitments in a canter, or what the president says about witch hunts, Mother Nature has switched into payback mode.

We are being punished for listening to, or ignoring, the psychopaths. They're mainly men, they're mainly white, they're mainly religious, and they're all damaged. But, we the enablers, the ones who have let them get their way, are of all different genders, skin colours and beliefs. We are the frightened masses and we vote them in, and it's hard not to feel at times that we deserve everything we get.

China did an experiment with population control, the one-child policy. It was a failure, and now any talk of population control is taboo. And while we're at it, because we here in the West can't even begin to comprehend the mind of China, we rule out collectivism and thus any left-leaning ideas and political policies. 'It's a slippery slope to communism,' the psychopaths scream when any murmurs of equality manage to gain some traction among the normally compliant enablers. Individualism facilitated by capitalism rages out of control.

Have you heard this: 'Climate change is an opportunity for jobs and growth.' Did you bang your head against a wall when you heard it? Or did you just shrug and think, yes, I guess it could be?

It's predicted that the human population on Earth will hit eight billion in the next decade: the Roaring Twenties? China won't do another experiment with population control. And here in Australia, population growth is essential for economic growth and prosperity, unquestioned.

As is foreign investment. So while we recoil at the dictatorial authoritarianism and the atrocities against human rights being committed by our communist neighbour to the north, we squabble about the tricky negotiations and balancing act required to maintain our trade with China and our unquestioned alliance with the USA, where they just impeached their psychopath president.

But all of this is human noise, pointless chatter. We don't need a human population control policy, or new emission targets to limit global warming to whatever number of degrees Celsius are agreed upon in Kyoto, Paris, or Madrid. Mother Nature is getting on with the job, restoring balance – we won't have to lift a finger.

So Deep in Story

When Kat gets back after seven years in Europe, she visits her mother. And the feelings return the moment she walks up the front path and spots her, standing at the front door. Feelings she can't articulate into words. Horrible, unsettling feelings.

She brings along her boyfriend, Fritz. He was born in Belgium and speaks a rare dialect of Flemish which he doesn't want Kat to bother learning. Together they are learning Spanish. There is a plan to live in Spain, on the Mediterranean coast.

The mother has tea and biscuits waiting on the dining room table. She says to Fritz, 'You are so handsome,' and then to Kat, 'You know your father was a handsome man. He used to model for David Jones in the city.'

'I know, Mum,' says Kat. She is regretting coming already. But she needs some paperwork that is hopefully still in her old bedroom.

Kat excuses herself from the table. She has warned Fritz many times about her mother and how she has a story for everything. She knows Fritz well; he will handle the mother, no problems.

Kat's bedroom is a time capsule. Nothing has changed. She finds her birth certificate and the academic transcripts from her degree in psychology.

A talking Bugs Bunny is propped up against the pillow on Kat's old bed. It doesn't work any more.

'What's up, Doc?' asks Kat. She wishes it could tell her. She tries to remember the toy's other expressions. She picks it up and pulls the string. Nothing.

There are lots of things Kat has forgotten about her childhood. But she'll never forget the disappointment when she opened up her birthday present expecting a Chatty Cathy doll only to find a rabbit. Her mother hadn't listened to her at all. Kat knew that much at least. She had tried in the past to diagnose her mother, especially when she was doing her psychology degree. The old biddy didn't seem to fit into any category at all.

Kat has to get out of the place. She goes back to the dining room and hears her mother telling Fritz all about Europe and its problems. The sick feeling in her gut and the tension in her shoulders increase.

'Thanks for the tea, Mum. We've got to go.'

'Oh no! Really, dear? You just got here. I haven't see you for seven years.'

'I know, Mum. I've got to get some copies of these and send them off.' Kat waves the papers in the air. 'Fritz and I'll come back soon and take you out for the day.'

'That'd be lovely, dear.'

In the car, Fritz says, 'You are right, Kat. Your mother is odd. Something not right. She is not in the moment.'

'You're not wrong there.'

'Was she like this before your father left?' asks Fritz.

'I don't know, I was only five. I can't remember what Mum was like before that. I've tried, and I've asked my uncle, Mum's older brother. But he's just like her. He gets off track and starts telling stories.'

'Ah…maybe grandparents have to do with this?'

'Maybe.'

Kat has heard a million stories about her mother's childhood. They are narrated like chapters from a poorly written novel, historical fiction at its worst. It's all drama and romance set in the rich red volcanic soils of rural Queensland. Kat's grandparents and a smattering of great-aunts and uncles play the pioneer roles. Heroic, inventive, resilient, hard-working, larger than life and thus without life. One-dimensional characters, needed for the sake of context. Then there's Kat's mother and her brothers and sisters. They're all still alive, spread around the globe and not having much to do with each other. Kat only really knows the one uncle, Harold.

Kat's mother's version of the family is at odds with what Kat has heard from other relatives. Uncle Harry has his version of events and his daughter, cousin Penny, has yet another version. Kat gets on with Penny. They are the same age and both fled their homes as soon as possible. Penny went to Perth, Kat went to London and boasts, jokingly, how she won in the 'creating distance' department.

Kat and Fritz have friends who own a boat that is moored on Lake Macquarie. It's a big boat and Charlie and his partner Chloe have invited the couple to come up for a day out on the water. They can bring one more person if they'd like. It's not as though Kat's mother has been hassling her, but Kat did say she'd take her mother out for the day soon. It has been three weeks since Kat picked up the paperwork from her mother's house and she hasn't seen her since.

As soon as they all step onto the boat, before anyone could start to do introductions, Kat's mother starts telling the story of how her husband built Halvorsen cruisers at Bobbin Head on the Hawkesbury River. 'He was a first-class boat builder, and we honeymooned on Pittwater on a cruiser personally loaned to us by non other than Lars Halvorsen himself. He was Norwegian, you know.'

Not only had Kat heard this story many times before, she also knew it to be largely untrue. Lars Halvorsen died in 1936, long before Kat's father worked for the company. And Kat's father had no qualifications as a boat builder. He was just a handy bloke who happened to date a girl who was best friends with one of the Halvorsens' daughters. Kat's father told her this, and other things, on his death bed in a Melbourne hospital when Kat was nineteen.

Kat's mother never lets the truth get in the way of a good story. Some of the nearby guests listen and acknowledge the elderly woman. Some try unsuccessfully to join in.

Kat and Fritz leave the mother and follow Charlie up onto the flybridge.

'Your mother's a character,' says Charlie as he starts up the motor.

'One day you too might become a character in the story of how she cruised Lake Macquarie on a million dollar motor launch.' Kat's tolerance has run out already.

Charlie laughs. 'Family, eh? You can't choose them.'

It is a big boat and Fritz and Kat grab a beer each and move to the foredeck. The light nor'-easterly breeze cools Kat's flushed face.

'Let it be, Kat.' Fritz gently squeezes Kat's neck and leaning forward kisses her shoulder. 'Look at this. Bloody fantastic!'

'The sooner we get to Spain the better.'

Kat can't contemplate living in Australia. The island continent is not big enough for her to escape the presence of her mother. The mother has been all over the country. She knows every town. The mother has cooked every meal on the national menu. She knows who won every federal election since World War II, and why and how. Plus, her mother is only eighty-four. She could live for another twenty years, the old battleaxe. Kat needs an ocean to separate herself from the mother. She needs a different language, a different cuisine, a whole new political constitution and national history. Things that she can have for herself, without the mother stealing them from her.

Kat knows when she leaves for overseas again, this time to live permanently, that she will once again be a character in one of her mother's stories. 'My daughter Kat lives in Spain, you know.' And that is all Kat feels she is in her mother's world, a character in a story. Not a real daughter, who is listened to and cared about. Not a real person with feelings and emotions, and desires and needs – like a hug, or a Chatty Cathy doll. Kat is just fodder for the story.

'We have another. Stay here, I will be back.' Fritz takes the empty can of beer from Kat and heads off to the ice chest.

Kat looks out across the water. It is a beautiful scene, as good as anywhere on the planet. If only she could enjoy it, if only she could let go of the mother in her head. She can do that overseas, she can't do it here. She especially can't do it when her mother is on the same boat. Why did she bring her along? She knew her mother would annoy her immediately. Why spoil a day trip on a luxury boat on a world-class lake? But Kat does know why she invited her mother. Kat wants to be heard, just once. Kat wants her mother to ask, 'How are you?' Kat can't recall ever hearing that from her mother. And it eats at her.

Chloe comes up to the front of the boat and sits down next to Kat. 'Your mother just told me about the day you fell off your pushbike and got ten stitches in your head.'

'Oh yeah. I suppose she also told you how she then had a passionate affair with the handsome doctor who treated me.'

Fritz comes back with two cans of beer. 'Sorry about Kat's mother, Chloe. She goes on.'

'It doesn't bother me. It's a pity, though, that she can't just enjoy the boat and the lovely weather.' Chloe laughs to herself. 'I was trying to offer her a drink and I couldn't get a word in. She's still standing at the back of the boat where she got on.'

If you mention anything about work, she will tell you a story or two about work. Same if the topic of family arises: she has volumes of stories about family. Recount a holiday, she has been there, or she knows someone from there, or she knows a fact about that place's history or politics.

She is a compendium.

She is Kat's mother.

Charlie's planned spot to moor and have lunch is full. Boats are tethered to each other and a DJ is playing loud thumping music that echos off Pilbah Island. Young and beautiful people are dancing on the decks and drinking champagne. Charlie knows of another spot further north on the lake. He's going to have to open up the throttle for a bit, and he sends a message to Fritz to get a life jacket on Kat's mother. Just in case.

Fritz heads aft to sort out the life jacket situation. He is dutiful. He knows how Kat is struggling with being back in Australia. He knows that Kat feels guilty about not making more of an effort to try and have some sort of a relationship with her mother. He's told her that there are no laws regarding mother-daughter relationships. She can do or not do whatever she wants. She is an adult now and not a child. But the child inside Kat still yearns for connection. Her bucket of unconditional motherly love is empty.

Fritz tries to get Kat's mother to put on the life jacket. The boat is roaring now and planing. As the boat hits the wakes of other boats, water sprays up and over.

'My second cousin drowned in World War II,' she says as Fritz offers her a yellow jacket. 'George was his name. He and his family were being evacuated from Rabaul because the Japanese were coming. He was only seven and he was having a tantrum because his bicycle had not been put on the boat.'

'How about we put jacket on, then you tell me story.'

'George's father said they would get a new bicycle. George didn't want a new bicycle, did he? He wanted his bicycle. The one he had painted British racing green.'

'Oh well, you know kids.' Fritz opens the jacket up and presents an arm hole.

'Well, you don't have to tell me that. You know, Kat herself was not a stranger to the odd tantrum or two. You should've heard the ruckus when she didn't get the exact talking doll she wanted for her seventh birthday.'

Fritz detects a streak of nastiness. Fritz has no hope. Kat's mum is deep in story. He lowers the life jacket and waits. The boat is heading north, pointed at a channel marker that it needs to round.

Up ahead, another large motor launch is heading south and on a direct collision course with Charlie's boat. Charlie is waiting. The boat will no doubt see him soon and veer starboard. There are young people dancing on the foredeck of the approaching boat. The approaching boats stays on its course. Charlie sounds the air horn as a warning.

Hearing the horn, Fritz turns around and assesses the situation. 'Come on, let's get this on.' He raises the jacket again.

'Oh, I love that sound. It reminds me when we used to stay at Uncle

Jimmy's place down at Port Kembla. He wasn't a real uncle, you know. But he was like family.'

The horn sounds again.

Fritz takes Kat's mother hand. 'Come. We sit down.'

She shakes his hand away. 'I'll be fine, young man. I've got good sea legs.'

A second showing of nastiness, Fritz thinks.

'Here. Take.' Fritz pushes the life jacket into Kat's mother's stomach. She has no option other than to take it.

Fritz has done as much as he can. He heads up to the flybridge to see what is going on.

Charlie explains that the other boat has not yet seen him and how it is their responsibility, and not his, to alter course. 'I don't have much channel left on the starboard.'

Charlie sounds the horn again. By now the thumping bass of the music on the other boat is audible.

Fritz looks back. Kat's mother is still standing on the stern deck. She has, though, moved a few feet and is talking at a woman who is sitting on one of the bench seats. The life jacket hangs lifeless from her left hand. Her right hand is pointing up at Fritz.

Kat has never before mentioned to Fritz how her mother can be mean. She has often spoke about how her mother can't stand silence and has to fill it with words. But she's never mentioned this nasty streak. If anything, Kat has always praised her mother for being a kind person. A bit off with the fairies, a bit living in the past, but not mean. The fact that the mother was for most of Kat's life a single mother who had to work, and who always managed to put food on the table, has been cited by Kat as evidence that her mother could not be classified as a bad person.

Fritz is mulling over all this as Charlie contemplates the on-water situation ahead. Though Fritz never studied psychology at university, he has a good sense of why and how people become who they are. Though, to be honest, he had always been puzzled by Kat's 'mother issues'. Kat's need to be overseas, and her nervousness at seeing her mother again after seven years, didn't quite match the childhood that Kat had been able to remember. Now, he was in Australia and experiencing this eccentric storytelling woman first hand. Now, it was becoming clear. Kat's confusion about her feelings, and the fact she had forgotten whole chunks of her childhood, were because Kat had been neglected and abused. Not physically, but emotionally. Deeply wounded inside, no scars on the skin. Wounds that had never healed. Wounds that Kat didn't fully realise existed.

'Hang on, Fritz,' says Charlie.

Fritz comes back to the present. He sees the motor launch ahead bearing down on Charlie's boat. Fritz grabs onto the console and Charlie swings the boat hard to the port side to avoid a collision.

There is a scream from down below on the stern deck. Fritz turns round. The oncoming boat passes by, the young party people still oblivious, still dancing. Charlie kills the engine.

Kat's mother has gone. People move over to the starboard gunwales. They stare down into the deep.

It will take six months at least for the estate to be settled. At Fritz's insistence, Kat has been attending counselling. Not grief counselling, as one might expect after such a traumatic event, but a form of repressed memory therapy.

Kat and Fritz have moved into Kat's mother house at Long Jetty. It's Kat's now anyway. Kat is the sole beneficiary. It's hard being around all the mother's stuff, remembering with new insight what actually did happen in that house.

Stuff is slowly being sorted. The jolly volunteers in the Salvation Army truck come every second Thursday and take away what is not wanted.

Kat comes home from another counselling session. Fritz is digging a new vegetable patch out the back. They have decided to stay on for a while. At least long enough to grow some food. Spain is on the backburner. Fritz is liking Australia. Kat is waking up, healing.

'How it goes?' asks Fritz.

'Good. Today we discussed the reality that I'll probably never know why Mum was like she was.'

'You right with that?'

'*Jawel, natuurlijk.*'

The couple laugh together.

'I have an idea,' says Kat. She heads inside.

She returns with the talking Bugs Bunny that talks no more. 'Do you have a stake?'

'Yes. Stake I have.'

'Put this up on it.' Kat hands Fritz the toy. 'We're going to need a scarecrow.

The Endless Summer
28 January 2020

Late January, water fills the air.

Bugs swimming on human skin, grazing, nipping at dead epidermal cells, probing deeper for summer blood.

Overnight minimums equal fair weather maximums. Sound sleep, a psychotic dream.

The busyness of another year ramps up. Minors getting ready for term one of the prescribed curriculum, majors plotting a win on the economic battlefield, if they're lucky enough to be enlisted. Every minute counts, now we're paid by the minute. Every minute accountable.

Be productive, economic growth depends upon it. Economic growth trumps everything.

This year, like last year, autumn is cancelled. A brief influenza soaked winter, your only break.

The sweat on your brow, on your collar and between your thighs, the lubricant for having a go.

Ready?

On your marks.

Get set.

Go!

Home is a Person

When he's away, the days are so long. What to do with all this time?

When he's here, there's walks to walk, gardens to tend, and dinners to prepare.

And then, there are those intimate times, times of connection. Hours occupied.

She goes to the shopping centre, not for the social interaction, just to kill time. She walks slowly through the aisles, spotting goods from any nation you could name.

She will try to remember that ingredient in the Eastern European section in aisle four. What could that be used for? Google that later, if I remember, she thinks.

She spends some time in cleaning products. Normally it's a quick stroll through here. Grab some laundry liquid, perhaps some dishwashing detergent, and do I need more Gumption? Hey, they still make Ajax, oh the memories. And look here, Sard Wonder Soap now comes in a stick; well, there you go. She spots a three-pack of Pear's Soap; he loves that, just one of his idiosyncrasies that simultaneously annoys and delights.

He'll be home soon. He'll appreciate the soap and the Hungarian pomegranate juice. And she'll smell his neck and armpits, and she'll relax. Home is a person, she has worked out.

Life and Death Are Not Simple Matters
29 February 2020

On Leap Day, it is traditional to move around the place in small leaps and to eat frog legs for dinner. Frog leg eating has been banned due to the severe lack of frogs, due to the severe lack of reliable weather, due to the severe lack of humans doing anything about spewing megatonnes of carbon dioxide into the air.

The vast majority of people refuse to leap about on Leap Day. They say it is a ridiculous tradition. Mind you, the same people seem to have no problem with the worshipping of Gods and all the silly rituals that go along with that lark.

I am going to leap around the supermarket and delight in all the looks of vicarious embarrassment that will no doubt come my way. I will buy some kangaroo steak as a substitute for frog legs. With a bit of luck, there will be some other leapers around and we can nod knowingly at each other.

Another tradition of Leap Day is that it is the one day when women are allowed, encouraged even, to propose marriage. This happened to me sixteen years ago. I was leaping around down at the beach when one Aileen Richtenhofer leapt up to me and popped the question. I was carefree and liked her front, as well as several other of her perspectives, and said, 'Yes.'

You may think that my immediate positive response was an invitation for hell to enter my life. And I have learned – I even knew it back then sixteen years ago – that what you think is none of my business, and therefore, I don't care. I did it. I remember thinking, if Aileen Richtenhofer turns out to be a nightmare, I'll just get a divorce, no big deal. It was spontaneous and reckless and I ended up having the best eight years of my life, after Leap Day 2004.

Aileen loved to dance. She could jive and tap and waltz and contemporary like the very best. She brought joy to people's hearts and toes. No one could resist her force of dance attraction and whenever and wherever she moved to the music, the dance floor would fill in no time. And she could eat and drink like the very best as well. Oh, the dinner parties we had in our little shack down by the lazy river.

It's been eight years since Aileen departed this mortal coil. I don't blame the truck driver. He no doubt has his own hell to deal with as he sits out his sentence behind the walls down by the bay. Yes, he was speeding, and yes, he was chock-a-block full of pills, but he had a wife and kids and was a renter saving for a deposit. Life and death are not simple matters.

These days, I don't dance often. I haven't found a partner so electrically light on her feet. But every Leap Day, I'm out and about leaping around. Perhaps it's my protest at a world gone wrong, or perhaps I entertain the silly notion that out of the blue a woman will ask me to marry her.

Aileen Richtenhofer would approve.